Author and playwright **Swadesh Deepak** was born in Rawalpindi on 6 August 1942. After his MA in English Literature, he taught for a long time at the Gandhi Memorial National College, Ambala Cantonment. Following a period of illness from 1991 to 1997, when he had little contact with anyone other than his family and close friends, he made a momentous return to the world of letters with an autobiographical account of his illness, *Maine Mandu Nahin Dekha*, and the play *Sabse Udaas Kavita*. He received the Sangeet Natak Akademi Award in 2004. He has a total of 15 published books to his name including short-story collections such as *Tamasha*, *Baal Bhagwan* and *Kisi Ek Pedh Ka Naam Lo* and hugely successful plays such as *Court Martial* and *Kaal Kothri*.

In 2006, he left home for a walk and never returned. He has been missing ever since.

Jerry Pinto is a writer and poet based in Mumbai. His books include the novels *The Education of Yuri* (2023), *Murder in Mahim* (2017) and *Em and the Big Hoom* (2012; winner of the Hindu Prize and the Crossword Book Award); the non-fiction book *Helen: The Life and Times of an H-Bomb* (2006; winner of the National Award for the Best Book on Cinema); and two collections of poetry, *Asylum and Other Poems* and *I Want a Poem*. An acclaimed translator, Jerry has also published landmark translations from Marathi and Hindi, among them: Baburao Bagul's classic collection *When I Hid My Caste*; Sachin Kundalkar's novel *Cobalt Blue*; and the memoirs of Daya Pawar (*Baluta*), Malika Amar Shaikh (*I Want to Destroy Myself*), Eknath Awad (*Strike a Blow to Change the World*) and Swadesh Deepak (*I Have Not Seen Mandu*). In 2016, he received the Windham-Campbell Prize and the Sahitya Akademi Award.

Pratik Kanjilal is a publisher and columnist. He was the co-founder, with Antara Dev Sen, of *The Little Magazine*. He was for many years literary editor and editorial writer at *The Indian Express* and has also worked with *The Economic Times*, *Business Standard* and *The Wire*.

Nirupama Dutt is a poet, journalist, art and literary critic and translator based in Chandigarh. She writes in both English and Punjabi, and occasionally in Hindi. She is the author of *The Ballad of Bant Singh*, the biography of a Dalit activist and singer of Punjab. Her other books include her poetry collections *Ik Nadi Sanwali Jahi* (winner of the Punjabi Akademi Award) and *The Black Woman*; *Stories of the Soil* (a collection of landmark stories from Punjabi, in English translation), *Half the Sky* (an edited book of fiction by Pakistani women writers) and *Poet of the Revolution* (a translation of the memoirs and poetry of Lal Singh Dil). She has also translated a collection of poems by Gulzar, *Pluto*, into English.

COURT MARTIAL AND OTHER PLAYS

Swadesh Deepak

Translations by

Jerry Pinto

Pratik Kanjilal

Nirupama Dutt

SPEAKING TIGER

SPEAKING TIGER BOOKS LLP
125A, Ground Floor, Shahpur Jat, near Asiad Village,
New Delhi 110049

Published by Speaking Tiger Books in 2024

Court Martial was first published in *The Little Magazine*,
vol. III, no 5–6: *Bloodsport*

ISBN: 978-93-90477-62-3
eISBN: 978-93-90477-63-0

10 9 8 7 6 5 4 3 2 1

Typeset in Garamond Premier Pro by SÜRYA, New Delhi
Printed at Rahul Print O Pack

Contents

Introduction

> You and I always write tragedies. Our vision of life is tragic. How did you imagine, Swadesh, that just wanting to write would be enough? No. First you have to live with your characters for years, you must take part in their joys and personal sorrows. You will have to bleed with them, accept extensive damage to the self. You must forget your own personal sorrows first and only then will you be able to write their sorrows. You know all this. When your characters come to you with hands outstretched, your book will begin to be written and then, whether it is a big book or not, it will be one that will lead you to salvation. And this long desolation will end.
>
> —Nirmal Verma, speaking to Swadesh Deepak, as reported by the latter in *Maine Mandu Nahin Dekha*

I am not a regular play-goer, which is a shameful thing to admit since I live in a city that has a rich tradition of theatre, perhaps one of the richest in India. This is where

Sultan Padamsee started Theatre Group and Ebrahim Alkazi gave city audiences a look at Euripides and Lorca. This is where Vijay Tendulkar lived and where Vijaya Jaywant (later Mehta) developed experimental theatre in school auditoria, integrating the ambient sounds of trains rattling past into the soundscape of her productions. This is where Satyadev Dubey took Dharamvir Bharati's *Andha Yug* and turned it from a radio play into an epic production. This is where you could see a Gujarati double-meaning play on Saturday and a serious Tamil play the next day, if you so chose. This city was as much home to Annabhau Sathe and Ram Ganesh Gadkari as it was to Adi Murzban and Sohrab Modi, two stalwarts of the Parsi Theatre that was to influence and shape Hindi cinema in the city. And this is where the faithful Goan could go and see Konkani tiatr, one of Goa's most durable forms of artistic expression. This city is home to dozens of playwrights, as Ramu Ramanathan, himself a playwright, reminds me often. (Thirty-five in Vile Parle alone, he once said, if I remember rightly.)

Despite this *embarras de richesse*, I am not a regular play-goer. But I do remember watching Nadira Babbar's production of Swadesh Deepak's *Court Martial*. The armed forces of India are in the habit of saying that caste does not matter once you put on a uniform. There is only one caste, they say, and that is 'fauji'. To which the only answer is: Who cleans the toilets at the cantonment?

Court Martial is about caste and the army. The play was

certainly the thing here. It was the kind after which you don't remember a performance or a set. You remember the impact it had on you. You remember the totality of it, the intensity of it. It is the kind of resilient play that very few things can destroy.

I did not translate *Court Martial* here; it appeared in *The Little Magazine* and the translators must have struggled mightily with it. I remember its tonalities, the words ringing, the actors exulting, the audience battered. I translated the other two, and although there are those who will maintain that Deepak's claim to being a playwright rests on *Court Martial*, I find these two plays interesting in different ways.

For one, it seems as if Deepak has been interrogating notions of masculinity in many of his works. His stories are littered with men in various states of breakdown and many of them have father issues. His own relationship with his father seems to have been a troubled one if we are to go by his magnificent account of his mental illness, *Maine Mandu Nahin Dekha*, which I translated some years ago. He was made to carry letters between his father and his father's mistress, for instance, but his father also translated his stories into Urdu so faithfully and so well (presumably) that in some quarters Swadesh Deepak was thought of as an Urdu writer.

Man as economic agent was another recurring trope in many of his works; the idea of a man without the need to earn a living turns up in different books including *Mayapot*, his novel. That a man should be defined by his ability to earn a living seemed a problem to Deepak. He was interested in how men responded to adversity, to being under the threat of death, to being someone who had survived close contact with death. Courage was important to him, more than grace under pressure, panache under pressure.

Theatre generally presents us with people at an inflection point in their lives. They must choose, they must act in some way to keep the play going; but in failing to act, they often present us with our own sins of omission. In these plays, Deepak presents us with people at an intersection and standing against them is the Establishment in various and different ways. It could be the army, it could be the bureaucracy, it could be the police or even the apparat of feudalism, but in each one, the individual is called upon to act with a purposeful heroism.

His interest in masculinity does not mean he was incapable of creating interesting female characters. In *Sabse Udaas Kavita*, there are two brooding female presences. There is the bereaved mother who wants vengeance for her son's murder; and there is the young journalist turned revolutionary. The men seem to move through the landscape of these two animas who are caught in a battle against each other, a battle fought through the men they love. In *Kaal Kothri*, we have Meena the wife, whose patience is at an end with her husband whose love of theatre cannot pay the bills. You can see echoes from Deepak's own life. In *Maine Mandu Nahin Dekha*, his wife, Geeta rages at him: 'Do not speak to me in poetry. Poetry has destroyed you; poetry has driven you mad. I hate your

Eliot, your Yeats. I hate your Soumitra Mohan. Will poetry feed your children, or me?'

The first time I read *Sabse Udaas Kavita*, I remember the eerie feeling I had. There she was: the doctor from South India, Dr Vasantha whom we met in *Maine Mandu Nahin Dekha*. I had only half-believed in the real-life existence of Dr Vasantha. And now here she was, in a clinic in an unnamed tribal area, no longer a doctor, but a journalist. And the doctor? The doctor's name is Sukant, the name of Swadesh Deepak's son.

Sometimes the plays feel like elaborate gedanken, thought experiments in which a group of disparate people are put together and the results are recorded.

Here is another clue. Deepak writes: 'To distract yourself when in a state of mental tension, it is important to do something. I started to shave. But the characters beyond the monologue in *Kaal Kothri* began to surround me.

'Give us our lives. I cut my cheek. Blood in the foam. I put a pinch of powder on the cut and then started after the other cheek. The raving and ranting woman in the play said: Write down my name. I wrote it down. I cut the other cheek. And laughed—a middle-aged cowboy bitten on the cheeks by a girl in her teens.'

The middle-aged cowboy? You'll find him, another doomed lover, in the short stories. And so, I believe these plays must be read with *I Have Not Seen Mandu* and with the short stories which Speaking Tiger is also bringing out in tandem with this book of plays. They are a trilogy, the Deepak trilogy. They may bring you no closer to understanding the enigma of Swadesh Deepak but they provide an oddly consistent world, an addictive world.

Jerry Pinto
May 2024

Kaal Kothri

Translated by Jerry Pinto

Cast

Rajat: Actor
Kaul: Badri Kaul, Director
Rajiv, Mahendra, Kanta, Balwant: Kaul's crew members
Naveen Varma: Playwright
Mrs Naveen Varma: Playwright's wife
Meena: Rajat's wife
Angad: Rajat's son
Father: Rajat's father and Angad's Dadaji; unnamed
Shobha: Rajat's sister
Officer 1: Unnamed
Officer 2: Unnamed
Sharma: Kishore Chandra Sharma, the Culture Commissioner
Vasundhara: Interviewee
Dada: Unnamed

Act One

Scene 1

Rehearsal room.

Rajiv: Have you read the new play? Did you like it?

Mahendra: Yes, I read it. I was suddenly a child again, a child grappling with a dictionary. God, the language! A flood of words, a veritable flood. It will drown us. And the audience too.

Kanta: I read it twice. I didn't even understand the subject.

Mahendra: That's because you're beautiful.

Kanta: What is that supposed to mean?

Mahendra: Beautiful women are generally stupid. Beauty and brains seldom go together.

Kanta: Watch your step. You're the limit!

Mahendra: It was God who crossed all limits in the making of you. Anyway, who are we to like or dislike the subject? The director liked the play. That's it. We are toys, mechanical toys. Kaul Saahab will turn the key. And we will mouth our lines.

Rajiv: Boss, are you an actor or a critic? The critics either murder the writer or declare him a genius; no middle ground. I know that writers are a little more idealistic than is strictly necessary. But there's definitely something in this play.

Mahendra: What?

Rajiv: No idea. I haven't got it yet.

Mahendra: And you won't get it either. The age of idealism has passed. But the characters in this play are all committed to their principles. They will give their lives for their ideals. But don't you worry, just go on brown-nosing Kaul Saahab. He'll give you a big role.

Kanta: Mahendra, there are times when you can be really evil.

Mahendra: I am evil; that's why I do theatre. My family abuses me regularly; if I do this play, the audience will join the chorus. Take it from me.

Balwant: Rajatji hasn't showed up yet? Let's see what he says.

Mahendra: Oh, he'll turn up. He'll turn up late, as always. Kaul Saahab has made him into a hero. Long speeches. There goes Rajat, yap, yap, yap. There goes the audience, clap, clap, clap. He must have loved the play. On every page, the protagonist delivers a sermon.

Balwant: Rajatji is a fine actor.

Mahendra: He is. A very fine actor. And we? For five years we've been lending our asses. Sometimes as a walk-on sentry, and if we're in luck, even a line to speak. And can you please stop this 'Rajatji-Rajatji' business? Even in his absence, you sing his praise. Why not buy some prayer-beads? You can chant his name as you tell the beads. He's our head honcho, our chief.

Kanta: Do I detect an additional note of bitterness today, Gandhari?

Rajat enters. Everyone welcomes him.

Rajiv: Read it? What did you think?

Rajat: It's going to kill us. Any which way, it'll kill us. God above! The writer has verbal diarrhoea. Even Hamlet would be turning in his grave.

Rajiv: Then why does Kaul Saahab want to do this play?

Rajat: He felt sorry for the writer. He said that the poor guy has written ten plays and not one has been staged.

Mahendra: Shouldn't he feel sorry for us? For the audiences? Will you talk to him?

Rajat: I will. I certainly will. Whatever else we get or don't get, we need to get some satisfaction from the work we do, right?

Mahendra: You'll get the hero's role.

Rajat: Oh, go on, play the hero yourself. Take the rotten tomatoes.

Kaul enters.

Kaul: So, have you all read it? What did you think?

All are silent.

Kaul: Come on, guys, be honest. If we aren't convinced about it, how will the play work?

Mahendra: Sir, the language is very difficult.

Rajiv: A whole bunch of ideals. All the characters are talking heads for the ideals they espouse.

Rajat: The hero's speeches are very long.

Kaul: When did you begin to fear long speeches? Often, the first reaction to a play is negative. Do you know where *Waiting for Godot* first resonated with the audience? In a jail in the USA, when it was performed for prisoners.

Rajat: We'll have to do this play in some in some jail too. At least we'll have a captive audience.

Mahendra: Sir, Rajatji says you're doing this play because you felt sorry for the writer that he's written ten plays and none have been staged. (*In a theatrical voice*) Why don't you feel sorry for us? What terrible crime have we committed to merit this dire punishment? Can't you choose another play?

Kaul: Bring me one. Where are the meaningful plays? No one's writing them. All of the writers are prostitutes to their politics. They do not wield pens, they wield lathis. All their characters huddle under the ragged party flags. Then there's the other kind: the products of the *Ramayana-Mahabharata* industry. We should write about the myths but make them speak to contemporary life. Make myth into metaphor. But no. Here our playwrights are subject to seizures. First they seized upon Kabir; now it's Karna's turn. I would never stage plays with such false mythic values.

Balwant: Sir, plays should be free of politics.

Kaul: Certainly, they should be free of sloganeering. But they must speak to the politics of life. People won't tolerate the old sophistries. The audience has become discerning. When they unseat governments, why should plays be spared? Let it go, let's talk about the play at hand. Rajat, read the concluding part of the speech.

Rajat opens his file.

Rajat: Let me tell you a story from the Jataka. Lord Buddha was delivering a sermon, saying that we can never escape the consequences of our actions, and there arrived a woman with her dead child in her arms. Sobbing, the grief-stricken mother asked Lord Buddha, 'Bhagwan, what sins could my son have committed in his short life? What actions of his could have merited the death sentence? If you are God, restore my child to life.' Even the gods must respond to a mother's grief. His eyes filled with tears, his lips curved in a gentle smile. 'Mother,' he said, 'bring me a pinch of ash from the hearth of a home that has not been visited by death. And I will revive your son.'

A very old man enters, his wife helps him enter the room. Kaul goes forward, takes his hand, sits him down in a chair. The old man is breathing heavily; he is practically gasping. His wife sits down next to him. Kaul gives him a glass of water.

Kaul: (*To all*) This is the playwright: Mr Naveen Varma.

All offer greetings.

Naveen Varma: (*Responds with a namaskaar*) I heard you were doing my play. I wanted to come and see my play in rehearsal. So, I came to your city against medical advice. What did all of you think of my play?

An awkward silence.

Naveen Varma: (*Taking a sip of water*) I know you won't have liked it much. I have written ten plays. I have come to the last stage of my life but not one of them has been staged.

The critics think me a fool. 'He's still carrying around the corpse of his ideals,' they say. When did ideals become such a bad thing? The future takes birth from the womb of the ideals of the present. Perhaps I will be able to see one of my plays performed before I set out on my final journey, thanks to your kindness. (*He gets up.*) If you don't mind, I will come to see rehearsals. I will enjoy that tremendously. I will take your leave now. I don't want to delay your rehearsal.

Kaul helps him up. His wife lends a hand too. All of them rise and make their namaskaars.

Kaul: I'll be back. I'll accompany Varmaji downstairs.

The three exit. An awkward silence.

Rajiv: He can barely walk.

Mahendra: Even sitting down, he can't talk without losing his breath.

Balwant: Not much time left.

Rajat: He'll die and he'll take us with him. Oh yes, he will.

Kanta: But he had a point. Why are ideals so wrong? The future is born from the womb of the ideals of the present.

Kaul enters.

Kaul: The stairs knocked the breath out of him. He should not have left his town. So, now you know. You've seen him for yourself. How the critics can slay a writer who is not a member of their clique. Naveenji is seventy years old. He has never received any notice for his work. Not a line written about him because he has never aligned himself with any clique.

All are silent.

Kaul: One must always approach a text with sympathy. Let us try another scene. Kanta, read the lines where the wife rages against her playwright husband who wants to bring about social change through his plays.

Kanta: Lock us all up in the dungeon of your ideals. Stick us all in a cell on Death Row. We must all be sacrificed to your ideals...

Kaul: You are talking like a lover. You need to speak as a wife would, a wife turned harpy by the hunger of her family. She now sees theatre as the other woman in her life. She does not hate her husband as much as she hates the theatre. Theatre is her Enemy Number One.

Mahendra: What would Kantaji know of how a wife speaks, she hasn't got married yet?

Kanta: Then you try it. You are married.

Mahendra: Sorry, boss, I can't demonstrate. My wife does not fight with me...

All shout: 'Lies!' 'Such rubbish.' 'A wife who does not fight?' 'Impossible!'

Mahendra: Boss, we have a perfect understanding. I make the big decisions; she, the small ones.

Balwant: Decisions? What decisions?

Mahendra: How to resolve the tension between India and Pakistan, how to deal with inflation, how to sort out the Ram Janmabhoomi issue in Ayodhya...all these are my responsibility. The small things...when to buy a colour television, which schools do we put the children in, which relatives do we visit—these are the decisions my wife makes. So why would we fight?

Suddenly, a power cut.

Kaul: Rajiv, can you check if it's a power cut or our fuse has blown.

Mahendra: We are theatrewaalas. Our fuse stays blown.

Kaul: Be serious for a change. There is no role for a joker in this play. Get some candles.

Mahendra: Yes, sir. The electricity comes like the Government of India and departs like the Government of India.

Scene 2

Rajat's home.

Meena, Rajat's wife, enters, carrying a burning candle. Rajat is seated, his head bowed. Meena squares off with him, in a terrible temper. She is standing.

Meena: That's right, starve in the name of art. Keep doing theatre. If you can manage nothing else, how about a length of rope? Enough rope to hang four people. That might be cheaper than food for four and a happier solution.

The electric current is restored.

Rajat: Meena, softly. You'll wake everyone up.

Meena: Who is asleep? Have you ever heard of hunger

bringing sleep? Charitable Karna. Keep giving away whatever you have on the stage, down to your kavach-kundal. For God's sake, think of the end of the month. You could have kept your word and brought some food. I had to borrow money from the woman who washes up to buy rice.

Rajat: She's not some stranger, nor is it the first time we've had to borrow. We'll return the money. What do you have to get all het up for?

Meena: My self-respect. My sense of self. Now I have to ask the servants for money for food! The servants.

Rajat: So, if you had asked a rich person instead, would you have merited a Padma Shri? We've only borrowed money. We'll return it.

Meena: Have you an iota of shame left? Such a big actor, a thespian of the stage and his wife is forced to borrow from the servants. If you couldn't afford it, why get married?

Rajat: I don't see the connection between borrowing from a servant and getting married. Have you started writing *akavita*, what they call unpoetry? We got married because we wanted to, you as much as I. I didn't abduct you against your will. We did the whole marriage thing, saat pheras and all.

Meena: You! Abduct me! What is this, some throwback to dialogues from a play about Prithviraj Chauhan? You do know that there's a difference between the stage and real life? A deep and terrible difference. But how can I blame you? You have no life of your own, no thoughts of your own. These dead characters from the pages of history have taken control of your mind. My younger sister was smarter than me. She married the man our parents chose for her. And now she lives the good life. Do you know what my mother said to me when I insisted I would marry you: 'The smart crow ends up sitting on muck.'

Rajat: Yes, your sister must be living the good life with Mr Military. He probably parades in bed too. Listen, my love, calm down. Why are you dragging your poor sister into our battle?

Meena: Life is not a play in which each one of us has a set of lines to speak in a scene. But you? How will you understand this? Your life is not your own, your words are borrowed. You have a life on loan, so you would mouth words that are on loan too. But reality is not a play or a stage that will change according to your whims. Reality is marriage. Reality is family. Reality is Meena. Meena, the woman who borrows from the servants.

Rajat: If you know so much about reality, if you're so wise, you should not have married me.

Meena: Truth then was limited only to the body and by the body. At that age, a young woman can find pleasure even in sleeping with a pillow. At that age, a young woman thinks with her body, not her mind. Those few minutes of physical pleasure become the ultimate pleasure. And then she must spend the rest of her life in tears, a life of begging.

Rajat: And love? I was not working even before we got married...

Meena: Don't use that word: love. It is a mockery, a foul thing. What was love for me? Sitting in the darkness of a cinema hall and holding hands? Meeting in parks? Lying with you in a bed borrowed from one of your friends. Do not utter that word: 'love'. I hate it...hate it. If for each time I slept with you I had hired myself out, I would have my own bungalow, my own car. Do you know what loving one man means? A house on rent. A life that stinks. Love is a bloody misunderstanding between two fools.

Rajat: Don't be vulgar. You don't see any difference between a wife and a prostitute?

Meena: Oh yes. There's a difference. Of course, there's a difference. A wife has a licence to sleep with just one man and she becomes cook, cleaner and baby-making machine. The prostitute meanwhile wanders through five star hotels. Don't keep talking about marriage. Bloody licenced prostitution.

Rajat: Got any money? I've run out of cigarettes...

Meena: Forgot your next line? Is that why you thought of cigarettes? What kind of a man are you? You don't even get angry. And you can't even beat me. People are right. A man who lives on his wife's earnings—his soul is emasculated. He becomes a pimp. And after a fight, you're always excited. Should I take off my clothes? (*She unfastens a button on her blouse.*) Would you like a cigarette now or after you lie with me, Rajat Saahab, you bloody great stage actor.

A boy enters the open door and sits down next to Rajat. The boy will enter in darkness. No one must see him enter.

Angad: Papa, has the new play started? Why didn't you take me to the rehearsal?

Rajat: Kaul Uncle has not started rehearsals yet. Tomorrow, I'll take you with me.

Angad: Promise, Papa? But please don't play Duryodhana. The boys tease me afterwards.

Meena: Son, can you imagine your father playing Duryodhana? Has he ever had anything to give away, even the head of a pin, never mind giving five villages?

Angad: How can you talk like that, Mummy? Papa, tell her something.

Rajat: Give me a cue.

Angad: Papa, from battle...

Rajat: *Arre baba*, don't say 'Papa', call me Duryodhana!

Angad: Duryodhana, if you can give nothing else, at least give the Pandavas five villages. Beware of war.

Rajat turns his back and raises his hands to his face. He turns. His body takes on an aggressive stance, his eyes flare with pride. He will deliver the dialogues that follow in the style of the Parsi theatre.

Rajat: You may be a God for those Pandava beggars. Go play your flute and dance with your Gopis. Look how you fear the threat of war. Have you ever raised a sword? Do you know its weight in your hand? Do you think to use the threat of war to make me hand over five villages? I will not give them even enough land to stand a needle on.

Angad begins to clap.

Meena: Do not plant these rotten dreams in my son's head. Do you want him to be an actor as well? You won't live in peace, nor will you let others live in peace.

Angad: Do that scene from *Chainpur ki Daastaan*, the one in which a man becomes a tree.

Rajat: How can we do that one? If I tell the story, who will react? You need two or three people at least.

Angad: Mummy, you do it with me. We'll jump about.

Meena: Not on your life! I can't act.

Rajat: Come on, love. For Angad's sake!

Meena and Angad stand up. Rajat does the night scene, and as he says 'Dhatt tere ki', Angad hops about on one foot because he is lame.

Rajat: We were walking about in a garden in the evening.

Angad, Meena: (*Jumping forward*) Really?

Rajat: When a letter fell from a tree.

Angad, Meena: (*Jumping*) Really?

Rajat: The people had all become trees.

Angad, Meena: (*Jumping backwards*) You don't say!

Rajat: The trees wanted to talk to us.

Angad, Meena: You don't say!

Rajat: I gave them an appointment.

Angad, Meena: (*Jumping forward*) Now that's too much!

Rajat: (*Angrily*) So, I'm lying?

Angad claps and helps Meena to sit down on a chair. She is breathing heavily.

Meena: Angad, you didn't hurt yourself jumping on one foot, no?

Angad: (*Also panting*) Not at all, Mummy. I even forgot I am lame. (*Turning to Rajat*) Papa, buy me a been.

Rajat: A been? What will you do with a been?

Angad: I will play it. That's what the lame do. They play the been.

Rajat: Who told you that?

Angad: (*In a frightened voice*) Papa, in school when they see me limping, all the boys sing—'*Langad, been bajaaye been.*'

Rajat drops a lit cigarette on the floor. He crushes it underfoot.

Meena: Angad, go and change your clothes. Your grandfather is coming over. Then we'll eat.

Angad limps out. Meena takes out a cigarette from the box and puts it to Rajat's lips. She puts a matchbox into his hands. She raises Rajat's head. He lights it and takes a deep drag.

Meena: Why do you always lose heart in front of the child? Schoolboys always tease each other.

Rajat comes to stand near her.

Rajat: I am a dog, a eunuch, a bastard. Why don't you hit me? Hit me.

Rajat takes her hands and hits himself with them. Across the face. She pulls her hands away and pushes him down onto the chair. She brings his head to her stomach and strokes his shaking back.

Meena: Don't cry, Rajat. Please don't cry. For God's sake, be brave.

Rajat raises his head. Meena wipes his face with her sari. At this moment, Rajat's father, a retired accountant, enters.

Father: What is it? What happened?

Meena: Nothing, Papa. Perhaps Rajat Saahab had a speck in his eye. I was trying to get it out.

Father: (*To Rajat*) If you've got something in your eye, splash it with water. Don't you know that much at your age?

Exit Rajat.

Father: There's no wind blowing, no dust flying. How did this speck find its way into Rajat's eye? Surely you must have...

Meena: I said nothing to your beloved son. The boys in Angad's school teased him calling him a cripple. He told Rajat about it and...

Father: Betaji, one day something will happen to Rajat. When a man is being kicked about by the world, he should find comfort at home. I know my son well. He pretends to be tough. But he has been sensitive from childhood. He will take all the beating you can hand out but he can't bear cruel words. Never mind. Let it go. It must have been a speck in his eye, as you said. (*He puts a hand in his pocket and takes out an envelope and proffers it.*) Here's some money. Keep it.

Meena: Money. It's the first of the month...

Father: The factory whose accounts I look after declared a bonus. A happy coincidence. This time they gave it to the workers and to the part-time workers like me...

Meena: What a life! You don't get to rest even after retirement. Every morning, you have to get up and go on your rounds, to the schools and factories, to look after their accounts.

Father: Betaji, has anyone died of working? Indolence is the body's greatest enemy. If I don't work, I'd end up lying in a charpoy, coughing.

Meena: You forgot to teach this to your son. His life is a fine one. Someone else earns and he gets to eat.

Father: It isn't physical work that tires us as much as mental work—thinking. Just think about it. It is bad enough to bear one sorrow but consider how many sorrows Rajat has to bear. Oedipus is blinded, Lear must wander on the blasted heath. Sometimes he must play Colonel Surat Singh and sometimes Rajat must linger, waiting for Godot. Who knows what curse makes one end up a stage actor? No amount of penance will ever end the curse.

Angad enters. He plants a foot firmly on the ground.

Angad: Lankesh, is there anyone here brave enough to lift my foot?

Father: (*Bowing*) I am Meghnad. I will not just raise your foot, I will pick you up and throw you out of Lanka.

Angad: (*Teasing*) Hey, old man, if you can't summon up the strength then you might want to take some. Plus 30 tablets like that film actor, Jeetendra.

Father: Buddy, that's not fair. You change the dialogue as you want. How is the other actor to respond?

Angad: Dadaji, the other day Kaul Uncle explained it to us. If a good actor forgets his lines, he improvises. That's improv—you can say what you want.

Father: No, my friend, you can never say what you want. What did you say to Papa today?

Angad: Nothing much, Dadaji. It's my leg that isn't working but Papa gets angry about it.

Father: Do you know why he named you Angad? He had such strength in one leg that no one in Lanka could shake him. God was not a fool to give us two hands, two feet, two eyes, two ears. If one is damaged, we can work with the other.

Angad: (*Settling his foot down again*) Go on, Raavan, try it. Raise my foot. Did you think that abducting a weak woman would make you a warrior? Try to raise a man's foot instead.

Rajat, in the doorway, overhears these lines. He takes his son by the hand and sits him down in a chair.

Rajat: Buddy, you should not see so many Amitabh Bachchan movies. You're always growling. You say whatever comes to your head. How will you become an actor? You cannot remember your lines. When Raavan rises to try and move Angad's foot, Angad stops him. Where did these filmy lines get in?

Angad: (*To himself*) Why do I keep forgetting the lines?

Father: You're still young. Try and learn the wee lines. You won't be able to recite long speeches as your father does, not yet.

Kaul, in the doorway, overhears these lines. Rajat looks in his direction and smiles.

Rajat: When did you get here, Kaul Saahab?

Kaul: I got hungry and turned up. Angad, go see if there's a banana or something in the kitchen.

Exit Angad.

Meena: Kaul Saahab, will you eat with us?

Kaul: Eat? Of course I'll eat. You've lived with Rajat for ten years and you haven't yet learned this small truth: that when theatrewaalas come over, they do not leave until they have eaten. And to add to my woes, my half-wife is ill.

Father: Half-wife, Kaul Saahab?

Kaul: My fridge, sir, my fridge. Cook something and stick it in there. Eat it over the next two or three days. Now, isn't the main duty of a wife to feed her husband? The fridge...

Father: But still, a half-wife...

Kaul: You only get food, sir. You can't sleep with a fridge, can you? So that's half a wife.

Father: You theatrewaalas are a crude lot. What weird connections you make!

Exit Father.

Meena: Dinner will take some time. Right now...

Kaul: I knew it. I saw it for myself. There was probably a Mahabharata being fought and Rajat was showing his histrionic skills so I asked Angad to get me a banana from the kitchen.

Enter Shobha. She has some packages in her hands. She makes her entry waving these.

Shobha: United made it happen. Everyone wins, everyone has a ball. Eat up, eat up and sing the praises of United.

Meena: All this stuff? Right now...

Shobha: Meena bhabhiji, I am a government servant, a government servant. I don't work for some tuppenny-ha'penny establishment. We got our Diwali festival advance. Eat up, eat up, United made it happen...

Kaul: Shobha, do you have your brains in your heels? You brought the chicken but forgot the accompaniments. No alcohol? You're chickening out.

Shobha: Of course I brought alcohol. I knew you would be here. Someone you know has to get a bit of money and the wind carries the scent to you.

Meena: What do you and your brother have against money? As soon as you get a little, you splurge. You ought to save some, invest some. Don't you want a house of your own? Or will you work till you drop like your poor father does to feed your parasite of a brother? Other girls your age have their hands painted with mehndi and you're applying it to your hair. You will get old and ugly before your time. Like me. Just like me.

Shobha: Meena, if you want to pick a fight, go find your husband. Don't make my marital status an excuse for a quarrel. You got married with your eyes open. You made your bed, now you must lie on it. Why do you always get angry if you see us having a bit of fun?

Meena: Your brother has turned me into a beggar. When a wife must live on the earnings of her retired father-in-law and her unmarried sister-in-law, how is she to take part in a bit of fun? My case is worse than that of a widow. At every step of the way, someone mocks me, insults me.

Rajat: Once in every while, try for a kind word. Are you a woman or a war machine?

Meena: My Lord and my All, may blessings be heaped upon you. I should sing your praises in the streets... What unlikely god had a hand in your making? And what unholy stuff did he use? Do you want a beggar to talk of roses? You expect sweetness and light from me?

Angad enters with Dadaji. He sees the roast chicken, and erupts in excitement.

Angad: Bags I the legs. Both legs are for me. I'm going to eat both legs.

Meena: Of course, sweetie. Both legs. Shobha Didi has thrown us some alms. Now you and your father may dine.

Angad: Mummy, whenever Shobha Didi gets her pay, she brings me chicken. And I always eat the legs. I'm going to eat them today.

Father: Why don't you begin? The problem with you theatrewaalas is that you never stop talking. You people are in love with your voices. (*No one says anything. They are all tense.*) Kaul Saahab, why don't you take the lead? Don't take it out on the food.

Rajat: Please eat, all of you. I am not hungry.

Shobha: Not hungry? Why aren't you hungry? Has her abuse blunted your appetite?

Meena: Shobha, behave yourself. Would I dare to abuse the great thespian, Rajat Saahab?

Kaul: Meena, please...

Meena: Why does the whole house revolve around Rajat? If his retired father is still working, it is to feed his actor son. His sister wastes the best years of her life at work so that Rajat Saahab may sit and dangle his legs...

Angad: The legs, the legs, I'm going to eat both legs.

Rajat jumps to his feet. He grabs Angad by the front of his shirt and pulls the boy towards him.

Rajat: Bastard, you have only one leg and you're going to eat both legs, bloody cripple...

Shobha stops the hand he has raised to strike the boy.

Angad: Papa, don't beat me. I won't eat the legs. I won't ask for a been.

Rajat lets go of his shirt. He grabs a corner of the table and upends it. The food falls on the floor.

Rajat: I'll give you a been. (*He starts towards Angad.*)

Father: (*Holding Angad close*) Come, son, let's go to our room. Your father has gone mad today. Shobha, come with us. Let these animals fight. Let them tear at each other's flesh.

Shobha: (*At the door*) Meena, you left a child hungry. Are you a mother or a witch? Take it from me, take it in writing. You will destroy them, my brother or your son.

Exit Father, Angad and Shobha. A short silence follows.

Rajat: Kaul Saahab, I will take up a job.

Kaul: Look, Rajat...

Rajat: (*Shouts*) I will work.

Kaul: Sure. Relax...

Rajat: (*Screaming now*) I will get a job.

Kaul: (*Gets up, goes to the door*) Okay. There is a vacancy for the post of a Deputy Director, Drama in the Lok Sampark Department. Apply for it. Interviews are on the 10th. The Culture Commissioner knows me. I am one of the experts on the panel. You will get the job. Bloody bastard, you hit Angad... I will get you this bloody job.

Darkness spreads across the stage.

Rajat: (*In a dead voice*) I will get a job.

Act Two

Interview room.

Officer 1: Sharma Saahab is late. The applicants have been waiting for three hours.

Officer 2: Kishorechand Sharma isn't only the Culture Commissioner, he is also an English poet. Inspiration must have struck. Oh, and by the way, don't speak too much Hindi in front of him. He will make a bad entry in your confidential report. He's a brown sahib.

Sharma enters. He is well dressed. His teeth protrude and he has the habit of licking his lips constantly. His English is impeccable, his Hindi suspect.

Sharma: Should we begin? Has Badri Kaul showed up? He's the expert, isn't he?

Officer 2: Kaul Saahab has been here for three hours. You were a little late so he went to the canteen for...

Sharma: Are you going to give me lessons in punctuality? Call him. And show me the list of candidates. Who is the most qualified of them?

Officer 1: Sir, experience and education would make Rajat...

Sharma: Why have you stopped? Keep it short.

Officer 2: There was a call from the Education Minister about Vasundhara...

Sharma: I got a similar call but we will choose the best candidate.

Kaul enters. Sharma rises, greets him, leads him to the chair next to his own.

Sharma: You know the remuneration for experts was abysmal. I got it raised from two hundred to five hundred rupees.

Kaul: Sharma Saahab, you are a veritable horn of plenty for us artists.

Sharma: Still the same mischievous tongue. Really, what would I be without all of you? Nothing. You are the ones who have kept the culture of this country alive. If only a few more IAS officers were culture aficionados, we could work miracles. Do you remember how I organized a culture festival in the capital? The late PM himself said: If only there were more ministers like Sharmaji... Never mind. Why live an impossible dream? (*To Officer 1*) Call the first candidate.

Vasundhara enters. She has short hair, a pleasing gait and a sweet voice. Whoever asks the question, she will look at Sharma and answer.

Vasundhara: Good morning, sir. Good morning, everybody.

Sharma: You have come to be interviewed for the post of Deputy Director. The department has many activities: dance, poetry festivals, theatre, looking after guests from abroad, et cetera. Would you be able to handle all this?

Vasundhara: I will try, sir. And then I am sure I will be the recipient of the guidance of art-loving officers like yourself.

Kaul: Could you describe what experience you have in this field?

Vasundhara: Sir, I travelled with the Festival of India to England, France and Germany. Now I have a wider experience of the world of art.

Kaul: What was your role in these festivals?

Vasundhara: Variety programmes...

Kaul: Sorry? What do you mean...?

Vasundhara: 'Variety programmes' means 'variety programmes'. Dance, music, bhangda, folk songs, et cetera. I could really entertain the people.

Kaul: Yes, I am sure you could.

Sharma: There are some critics who say we are a poor country. They feel these festivals should be stopped. What do you think?

Vasundhara: Sir, that's the problem with the Leftists. They always burn with jealousy when someone else does something. They think art and culture is their personal property. They hate the classics. They think art means only politics. In the last few years, the art and culture of our country has caused a stir all over the world. Why? On account of such festivals. They enrich our minds; they deepen our experience.

Sharma: Indeed, they do! John Donne says, 'No man is an island in himself.'

Vasundhara: Sir, what a fantastic knowledge you have of English poetry.

Sharma: (*Delighted*) I did my master's in English from Harvard. I topped the IAS but I decided that I would work for culture and art. Everyone writes in Hindi. I write poetry in English so that the world will know that Indians can also write poetry in English.

Kaul: What a favour you did to Hindi.

Vasundhara: I always read your writing, sir. Someday you will get the Nobel Prize. You have written so many poems on birds and trees. Everyone writes on human beings. But your concerns have transcended mankind.

Sharma: Do you like reading poetry? Who are your favourite poets?

Vasundhara: Sir, please don't mind, after you, T.S. Eliot is my favourite poet. Somehow or the other, Hindi poetry goes over my head.

Sharma: Why would I mind? (*To Kaul*) Do you have any questions?

Kaul: Stanislavski has propounded some theories about acting. Would you like to talk about them?

Vasundhara: Sir, I am a performing artist. I don't believe in theories but in practicals. I don't know as much as famous directors like you do. You teach these theories but we perform.

Sharma: (*To the two officers*) Don't you want to ask anything? Why are you sitting there, silent as stones?

Officers: (*Together*) Oh no, sir... When you are here...

Sharma: Go on. Ask her some general knowledge questions.

Officer 1: Our first Prime Minister's daughter's name?

Vasundhara: Mrs Indira Gandhi.

Officer 2: Name a famous tragedy by Shakespeare.

Vasundhara: *Hamlet*. *King Lear*.

Officers: (*Together*) Good. Very good. Your general knowledge is very good.

Kaul: In what plays have you acted?

Vasundhara: You might feel bad but I only do the classics. In *Oedipus*, I played the king's wife and mother. The pleasure of sleeping with the son ultimately becomes a heart-rending torture. I have also acted in some 'bold' plays. We have made a great deal of progress. We must come out of the age and problems of life described by Premchanda...

Kaul: Please leave 'Premchanda' out of this. Is there a scene from a play...?

Sharma: Move on from theatre, Kaul Saahab. The Lok Sampark Department has many other jobs besides theatre. (*To Vasundhara*) Could you demonstrate a little of that classical dance sequence which you performed in Paris? I myself was present. The French were spellbound.

Vasundhara: Thanks a lot, sir. I will try and do a few steps from that performance. Raudra and Shringara.

She stands up. She performs 'Raudra' looking at Kaul and 'Shringara' while looking at Sharma.

Sharma: You are really good.

Vasundhara: Thanks a lot, sir. May I go now, sir? When will the results be declared? We struggling artists...

Sharma: Do not say 'struggling artists'; it hurts me. We will let you know by tomorrow.

Vasundhara: Thanks. Thanks all of you.

Exit Vasundhara.

Sharma: She's good.

Officers: Oh, very good.

Sharma: Call the next candidate.

Officer 1: Sir, the next candidate is Rajat...

Kaul: Sharma Saahab. Rajat has been a theatre actor for ten years. He is a fine actor. He has acted in many of my plays. Moreover, he needs this job. Last year, you presented him with the Best Stage Actor award.

Sharma: Badri Saahab, I spend most of my life giving out prizes. Every artiste wants to receive a prize from my hands. How am I supposed to remember these insignificant events in the swing of my busy life? Why didn't you tell me that you theatrewaalas are facing economic problems? I would have figured out a grant for you. Let's see.

Rajat enters. His clothes are worn but clean. Sharma looks at him and his clothes for a moment and then tells him to sit.

Sharma: Your name?

Rajat: Sir, Rajat.

Sharma: That I know. You must have a surname like everyone else. I am Kailash Sharma, he is Badri Kaul. Why this half-name?

Rajat: We are half-men living half-lives in these times. Moreover, I do not believe in the caste system, so, only Rajat.

Sharma: Okay. (*Looks at the biodata*) You've acted in a number of plays. You must be used to a life of freedom; why do you need a job?

Rajat: Sir, I have a family. They must eat. They feel the pangs of hunger.

Sharma: (*Sharply*) The stomach. You lot never go below the stomach nor do you rise above it. A man is not a body alone. He has a mind, a spirit, a soul and all these combine to give us a total human being. Why do you limit hunger only to the stomach? What about the hunger for knowledge which is infinitely precious? Are we still in the Stone Age? The beauty of the unknown, the unseen and its relentless search should be the vital concerns of an artist. T.S. Eliot has said, 'The man who suffers and the artist who creates are differentiated.' It is only when we forget the pain of others and our own suffering that we can create a poem, or any creation.

Rajat: Yes, sir. But one cannot talk of moonlight and roses to a beggar. You cannot put a hungry child to sleep with fairytales. The search for beauty should be the concern of every artistic mind. But this must come after the stomach is filled.

Sharma: You haven't acted in *Ashadh Ka Ek Din* up to now. You probably did not like the play. The first drops of rain take Kalidas away on a painful journey.

Rajat: *Ashadh Ka Ek Din* is great, sir. But there are other sorrows in the world besides the parting of lovers. Those are important concerns for us.

Sharma: You probably don't care for *Waiting for Godot* either.

Rajat: *Waiting for Godot* is the century's most important metaphor. Living a life devoid of meaning, man waits for something good to happen. But the problems of our nation are not alienation and meaninglessness. They are hunger, the rising cost of living...

Sharma: Well, thank heavens you took the trouble to read the play. Tell me the spelling of Godot.

Rajat: G-O-D-O-T.

Sharma: If there is a 'T', why don't you say it?

Rajat: Sir, the 'T' is silent.

Sharma: Why is it silent?

Rajat: No idea, sir.

Sharma: (*Delighted*) Let me tell you why. I myself met Beckett in Paris. I had gone there to invite him to India. But to our nation's bad luck, he was ill and could not come. All the critics were scratching their heads trying to find out where the name 'Godot' came from. I asked him. Beckett himself told me that there was a jockey in Paris whose name was Godot. You know what a jockey is? A man who rides horses in a race. An actor must have some knowledge of themes, he must have a sense of history or his acting will be lifeless. He should have a critical sense as well.

Rajat: Yes, sir. You're completely right, sir.

Sharma: Why haven't your plays been sponsored by the state? Just a couple of shows, and then, before the critics' bouquets and brickbats have landed, you're done. Why?

Rajat: No idea, sir.

Sharma: I'll tell you why. There has to be a live contact between theatre and its audiences. Do some folk theatre.

Connect with the people. European realism is all very well and fine in its place. If you cut yourself off from your own culture and traditions, how will the audience appreciate your work? Experiments must be done. Oh yes. They must happen. Folk theatre with today's sensibility. Who was that director who presented King Lear in the Chhau folk art tradition? His name eludes me right now but it became a milestone in theatre.

Rajat: He was great, sir. Greater even than Shakespeare, who did not know that King Lear could be done in Chhau.

Sharma: (*To Kaul*) Ask something, Badri Bhai.

Kaul: I don't want to ask anything, sir. Rajat has acted in my plays. He is a very fine actor.

Sharma: He must be, if you say so. But an actor cannot be a responsible officer. (*To the officers*) Go on, ask something. General knowledge?

Officer 1: Marx's father's name?

Rajat: I don't know.

Officer 2: Macbeth's mother's name?

Rajat: I don't know.

Both officers: Such a great actor and you don't know much. Surprising!

Officer 1: None of your plays has gone abroad. They were not included in the Festival of India. Why?

Rajat: I don't know, sir.

Officer 2: No state government has sponsored one of your plays. Why?

Rajat: I don't know, sir.

Both officers: You seem to know nothing. Surprising!

Sharma: Bhai, you guys are asking the wrong questions. Someone who is an expert in a limited field is hardly likely to be a scholar. You would hardly expect a good washerman or an expert weaver to discourse on the Bhagavad Gita. Skill and experience in a narrow field of life can never make us great and complete men. Never mind. Acting. Let's talk about acting. You would be familiar with the characters you played. What role will you perform for us? A bit of instant acting.

Rajat: Instant acting!

Sharma: (*Triumphantly*) Improvization, bhai. Your English seems weak. According to you, the basic reason for the existence of art is entertainment.

Rajat: Yes, sir. If a nation that lives baking in the sun wants to get away from their woes and enjoy themselves for a while, what harm is there in that?

Sharma: No harm at all. No harm. No harm in perverting the people's minds in the name of entertainment. No doubt you admire Johnny Walker and Mehmood too. The favourites of the front benchers.

Rajat: Yes, sir. However they do it, they keep people happy.

Sharma: So go on then. Show us how those actors do it.

Rajat: Would you like to see drunk acting?

Sharma: Sure. If you can manage it.

Rajat rises, turns his back. He puts both hands on his face. After a pause, he turns, lurches and comes to stand in front.

Rajat: (*In a shaking voice*) You are great, sir, truly great. Do you know why? Because your name is suffixed by three magic letters—IAS. Kishore Chandra Sharma, IAS, Commissioner, Culture. Everywhere, we hear stories of your greatness. When you turned forty, there were special editions in the journals. When you turned fifty, the same journals sang paeans of praise. You are great, sir, truly great. (*In an ordinary tone*) Who other than you is so concerned about art and culture? You have magicked into being a rain of awards and turned artists into lap dogs—dogs who will wag their tales when patted, dogs who will keep wagging their tails when kicked. The only ones who escaped this metamorphosis were us theatrewaalas. Us bastard theatrewaalas, we have truly hard skulls. Do you know why we do not get state-sponsored shows? Because we do not know how to lick the feet of officers. (*His voice rises*) You too feel the pangs of parting, of sorrow, but only for cultural reasons. Thousands of people die in accidents but you are concerned about culture festivals. Why? Because culture does not halt for a few dead bodies here and there. (*Roars*) Your father, T.S. Eliot, the one whose praises you sing, do you know what he said about the basis of poetry and poets? It is not just a matter of beauty but the boredom, the horror and the glory. You are dead, soul-dead. (*He leans forward, grabs one of them by the kurta, hauls him to his feet.*) I am disgusted. If all you want is a massage, you should keep a mat and oil at hand if that is your pleasure. You assassin of the arts, your shit is rich in the arts, your piss is rich with the arts. Why are you silent? Why? Shall I tell you why? You are silent in the same way that the 'T' is silent in Godot.

Kaul grabs Rajat and drags him out of the room.

Act Three

Rehearsal room and stage.

Kanta: Take Act Two. Kaul Sahaab will be late today.

Mahendra: He's the subject expert. He'll make sure Rajat gets the job of Deputy Director.

Balwant: I read Naveenji's play again. Perhaps values and ideals aren't so bad, after all.

Rajiv: Buddy, you've just arrived in the Big Bad City. Wait a little, and then tell me what happens to these values you and Naveenji share. The competition here is cut-throat. Today, only the idealist can talk about values—the idealist or the fool. There's not much difference these days.

Mahendra: Great lines! Perhaps you should try your luck as a writer.

Balwant: I think we should read his play...

Mahendra: Shut up. Just shut up. You're stuck in a rut of your own making.

Kanta: Why don't you let Balwant speak? Stop getting after him. The play isn't that bad, it's just that there's something to it we haven't got yet.

Rajiv: Tell me when you do. Right now, let's just get on with Act Two.

Balwant: Who will play Rajatji's part?

Mahendra: Buddy, you fear Rajat too much. Come on, have some confidence in yourself. Or you'll find yourself out in the cold. Maybe you're right to fear him. What a man he is. Meena Bhabhi whips him with her tongue but he never complains.

Rajiv: Mahendra, what a shit you are. At least, leave his personal life out of it. Stop this Ramayana. Kantaji, let's get on with that scene.

Kanta: Right you are. Balwant, make your entry. Let's take it from the line about exposing the teacher. And Mahendra, take the place of the verminous teacher.

Rajiv: Kaul Saahab always gets his casting right. Vermin plays to type.

Mahendra: My friend, today you will pay for your own lunch. And I know you're broke. (*He sits down on the stool in the room and puts on a pair of spectacles.*)

Kanta: Start. Balwant, your entry please.

Balwant: The most terrible drought of the winter and we get television towers instead of tubewells so that the people can mainline religion: the opiates of the Ramayana and Mahabharata.

Mahendra: I know that a red flag burgeons inside you. One blow from the government will topple it.

Balwant: Masterji, the people no longer fear the government. They will have their rights even if they must seize them by force.

Mahendra: (*Stands*) Really? Who has marked out our countrymen as strong? The great poets and writers all come scuttling out of the shelter of the government and rush into the shadow of God. They start writing religious stuff...

An old man enters. His clothes are spattered with colour. The rehearsal stops.

Rajiv: Dada, have you forgotten? There's no show today. What good is your magic box today?

Balwant places a chair next to Dada. He sits down cross-legged and takes a puff of his beedi.

Dada: Didn't forget. I just came to see your monkey-faces. Not easy to go from being a beast to being a man. You go on.

Kanta: (*To all*) Can someone do Rajat's lines? Without him the scene...

Rajiv: Stand up and read his lines. He's probably got the speech by heart. What an amazing memory. Rajat isn't a man, he's an LP.

Meena enters, carrying a tiffin, and leading Angad by the hand. Angad lets go of her hand when he sees Dada. Dada uncrosses his legs and brings Angad to sit next to him. Meena puts the tiffin on the table.

Mahendra: What's in the box, Bhabhi. You must have brought kheer. To celebrate Rajat becoming Deputy Director. May I open it? Let the festivities commence.

Meena: I brought lunch for the great actor. He left for the interview without his wallet. He must have been hungry all day. I knew he'd come here first, to his temple.

Kanta: He left with no money at all? The interviews are at least eight or ten kilometres away. He must be walking here.

Angad: Mahendra Uncle, if Papa becomes an officer, he'll get a car, no?

Mahendra: Yup, buddy. A car and a bungalow, too. Now Angad Saahab will not travel to school on the bus. (*He sings*) He'll travel by car / He'll go very far.

Angad: Uncle, did you watch television yesterday?

Mahendra: Nope, buddy. Yesterday I was sucking up to your aunt. I took her to see a film. What did you see on Doordarshan?

Angad: They showed a programme on a hospital in Jaipur. A doctor had made a foot out of wood. The Jaipur foot. And with it, cripples may walk. It must be very expensive.

Mahendra: (*A little angrily*) How expensive can it be? (*To the others*) Say after me, take an oath: When this play makes us some loot / We'll get Angad a Jaipur foot.

Kanta, Rajiv and Dada repeat after him.

Angad: (*Clapping his hands*) You act so well, Uncle.

Mahendra: (*Solemnly*) That was no acting. It was a promise. I will take you to Jaipur myself.

Rajat enters. He sees the tiffin and heads straight for it. He opens it, pulls out the first roti and begins to devour it.

Meena: Stop. Stop a moment. Let me take out the daal and the veggies.

Rajat: Go on. Take them out. I'll eat them too.

He takes out the second roti and begins to eat it. Meena opens the other containers of the tiffin. She takes a spoon out of her handbag and offers it to him. Rajat picks up the container with the daal, swirls it about and begins to drink it, some of it drips on his jacket. Meena wipes it off with the edge of her sari and replaces the container. He grabs the third roti but this gets stuck in his gullet. Kanta hands him a glass of water. He drinks it and goes on eating.

Meena: What's the rush? Is someone going to steal your food? You'll choke...

Angad: Papa, are you very hungry? Didn't you have tea?

Rajat: No, son.

Angad: How did the interview go?

Rajat: Wonderful, great.

Angad: (*Happily*) Now I will go to school in a car.

Rajat's hand, moving towards his face, stops. He drops his hand.

Meena: Angad, we don't talk when people are eating. Let Papa finish his meal. He hasn't had a bite since morning. His Highness did not even have breakfast. Said he'd get late for the interview.

Through this whole scene Dadaji's eyes will be fixed on Rajat. He will keep smoking beedis.

Meena: (*Pushing the container to Rajat*) Eat one roti with the vegetables at least.

Rajat finishes that roti. He takes out a handkerchief to wipe his hands.

Angad: Papa, wash your hands. Om Puri Uncle comes on the television every day and says we must wash our hands before and after eating. If there's no soap, we should use ash.

Rajat goes out. Kaul enters.

All: (*Talking at about the same time*) How did the interview go, sir? Rajat will get the job, right?

Kaul: (*Harshly*) No. Is Rajat here? Where is he?

Kanta: He's washing his hands.

Kaul: Did you guys ask him about the interview?

Voices: No, sir.

Kaul: And don't ask, either. He was humiliated. Terribly humiliated. He grabbed an IAS officer by the throat.

Angad: (*Happy*) Papa beat him up, Uncle?

Kaul: No, he assaulted him. The officer wanted to file a police complaint. Rajat would have been in jail right now. I dissuaded him by saying it would cause a scandal. Do you know what those dogs asked him?

Meena: What?

Kaul: Marx's father and Macbeth's mother's names.

Mahendra: (*Forcefully*) Why?

Kaul: How do I know? Ask them.

Angad: Now I won't have a car...

Meena: For God's sake, shut up. Promise you won't ask Papa anything. Promise!

Angad: Promise, Mummy.

Dada strokes his head. Rajat enters.

Rajat: Kaul Saahab, you're here? Shall we start rehearsal?

Kaul: Right. Start with the entry of the drunkard Brahmin. The scene in which he abuses his wife.

Both take their positions.

Rajat: Three hours at the burning ghats, breathing smoke and ash and I must come home to cold rotis? And then she threatens to leave me. Don't you know the status of a woman? She's the chillum in the courtyard. Anyone can use it at their pleasure...

Kaul: Stop. Are you speaking your lines or reciting time tables? The 'status of a woman' line—say it with contempt, not anger. You have just beaten your wife.

Rajat: Don't you know the status...

Kaul: (*Cutting him off*) No, Rajat, not like that. (*He goes to the door, and in a voice filled with contempt and hatred*) Don't you know the status of a woman?

Mahendra: (*In a tone approximating Kaul's*) Don't you know the status of a woman?

Kaul: That's it. Say it like that.

Rajat: Sir, let Mahendra do the role.

Mahendra: (*To Rajat*) Sorry, sir, only trying to help.

Rajat: What did you say?

Mahendra: Sir, I only...

Rajat: Don't call me 'Sir'. If you call me 'Sir' again, I'll kill you. I will kill all the bloody Sirs of this world.

He drops into a chair, his hand on his face. In a shaking voice:

Rajat: Sorry, Mahendra, I am really sorry.

Kaul: Rajiv, order some tea. We'll take a break.

Exit Rajiv.

Dada goes to Rajat, offers him a beedi.

Rajat: No, Dada. Thanks.

Dada: Take it. Smoke it. Go on then.

He lights a beedi. Rajat takes a long drag.

Dada: No use living out your anger on the stage. No use bringing your grief here. You can only live the role and its feelings. You must murder yourself to be an actor.

The chaiwaala enters. Everyone takes a glass of tea. Meena takes two. She gives Rajat one, puts a hand on his shoulder. She begins to drink. Enter Rajiv.

Rajiv: (*To Kaul*) Naveenji and his wife are coming.

Kaul: Good God, I thought they had gone. Come on, pick up your scripts. Rajat, that long speech?

Rajat: Not sure I remember...

Kaul: Read the lines.

Balwant: I know them. Should I?

Kaul: Go ahead.

Naveen enters, supported by his wife. All rise to greet him but with guilty looks. Kaul gives him a chair. Naveen sits down and folds his hands in a namaskaar.

Naveen: My apologies. I could not come for a few days. My spirit was willing but my flesh was weak. Today I thought I might come and watch a rehearsal of my play. (*To Kaul*) Kaul Saahab, please go on.

Kaul gives Balwant a cue. He stands up.

Balwant: Your children must also have given you endless grief. On the blasted heath, in the pouring rain and lightning, I am King Lear, that poor forked animal. But I...

Naveen: Kaul Sahab, have you changed the casting? I thought Rajat...

Kaul: (*Dismissively*) It happens. When you're actually doing a play, we try out different actors.

Naveen: I'm sure you're right. How many directors like you do we have? But would you mind if I offered a suggestion?

Kaul: Please.

Naveen: This section of the monologue should be spoken in a tone that suggests a state of near madness.

Kaul: (*Angrily*) No such thing. There is no madness here. It will come in stages. Now I know why your plays have never been staged. You don't know the A-B-C of stagecraft and you are setting out to teach me. Me!

Naveen: (*Getting to his feet*) Kaul Saahab, please forgive me I disturbed you. (*Looking at his wife*) We should go. (*To Kaul*) Please do what you think right.

His wife helps him out of the door. Kanta, Mahendra and Rajiv go with him. A small silence. Everyone's face shows their guilt. Enter Kanta with the playwright's wife. Everyone is taken aback.

Playwright's wife: Please don't get up. Please stay seated. I am only here to ask forgiveness on his behalf. I know you're not doing his play. That you have come this far, that you have taken even this much trouble, is more than enough. Just to keep him happy, you fake a rehearsal, you stage a reading. How wonderful you theatrewaalas are. You would not hurt a fly. Do you know, he has been in hospital for the last three days? When he was discharged, he insisted he must come for a rehearsal. So I brought him. I didn't even check with the doctor. Never mind. I'll take your leave.

Angad: Aunty, I'll come with you.

He gets up and limps over to her. She is stunned, shocked into silence. When he reaches her, she embraces him, begins to kiss his head and face. Startled, Angad retreats. At this she screams, a terrible scream of pain. She falls to the floor.

Playwright's wife: (*Wails*) My son, my son.

She begins hitting her own face. Meena rushes up and stays her flailing hands.

Meena: What happened to your son?

The playwright's wife breaks free and begins to pound on floor with her hands.

Playwright's wife: He died. My son, he died. (*Screams*) Our only child. He died, he died.

Her head on the floor, she sobs, her voice breaking. All are turned to stone. Angad brings her a glass of water. He sits on the floor. He raises her head and holds the glass to her lips. The water drips on her clothes.

Kaul: Go, one of you, go and bring Naveenji here.

Playwright's wife: No, don't call him. For the love of God, don't tell him anything...

Angad: Please don't cry, Aunty. One of my legs doesn't work. I never cry. So why are you crying? How did your son die?

Playwright's wife: He was your age when he lost both his legs in an accident on the road. And he wanted to become an actor. He had no will to live after that. He simply wasted away after that. This play was written in memory of his dead son. (*She kisses his head*) Don't you go and die, child—don't be as cruel as our son.

Angad: I promise, Aunty. I will not die. For my name is Angad. Who can kill me? Even the greatest of Raavan's warriors could not move a foot of mine.

Angad leads her to the door. After they leave, a stunned silence. Kaul comes forward and shifts the stool from the centre of the room. Everyone begins to move the properties of the play. They are rehearsing. And slowly the new set of another play takes its place. The actors gather in groups and then begin to speak.

Rajat: May I tell you a story from the Jataka?

Mahendra: Rajan, today on the battlefield...

Balwant: There is no cure and hence we must endure. The fire of grief scours us out.

And as they speak, the lights fade. Kaul goes to Dada.

Kaul: Dada, we're up in two days.

Dada: You will do it, Kaul Babu. You will certainly do it. You're theatre's top dog. You will do it. The last play closed in five...

Night. A single bulb glows. All lights on to indicate the arrival of day. The set will change to a new one and the actor's clothes will also change.

Kaul: Last speech. The English line.

Rajat: There is special providence in the fall of a sparrow.

Kanta: Sir, should we try this line in Hindi?

Kaul: Go on. Try it.

Kanta: *Nahin marti ek chidiya bhi, Prabhu ki ichha ke bina.*

Kaul: No, let's leave it in English. The rhythm of the

speech will be affected. Mahendra, your entry now. Rajat, take centre stage. Kanta, you're in the other doorway. A messenger has brought a message of disaster. You are turned to stone. Clear? Great. Start.

Mahendra: (*Entering via the door*) Rajan...

Kaul: Stop. You will not come in. The dwaarpaal never enters the king's...

Mahendra: Sir, you haven't completed the blocking.

Kaul: And what do you think I'm doing now, smartypants? Enter.

Mahendra: (*At the door*) Rajan...

Kaul sees that Rajat's hand goes to his face.

Kaul: Stop these Dilip Kumar-style mannerisms. You will have already turned your face to the door. You've already heard the footsteps of the messenger. You know he is coming with terrible news.

Rajat: I'm hungry. Any idea when...

Kaul: Are you hungry? Will you eat my brains? Rajiv, take someone with you and bring some packed lunches. This month we'll have to rough it out, no splurging.

Here the director must use lighting to indicate that it is now the evening of the next day.

Angad: Papa, I won't go to school today.

Rajat: Don't go.

Meena: Angad, you have afternoon school. I'll come and fetch you at five. The play will only start at seven pm, right? Shobha will bring you a new shirt tomorrow. A readymade shirt. You'll watch the play in new clothes.

Angad: Kaul Uncle, can I come to the make-up room?

Kaul: Sure, buddy. But right now, quiet as a mouse, okay? (*To Rajat*) Last lines of the speech, please. Take it from the Jataka.

Rajat: Let me tell you a story from the Jataka. Lord Buddha is delivering a sermon...

Kaul: Stop. This is the Buddha speaking. Peace, perfect peace. Speak like a saint. You have emerged from a river of sorrow. You are free now, free of happiness, free of pain. Have you heard Acharya Rajneesh's cassettes? That kind of voice.

Rajat: I will use my own voice, if you don't mind.

Kaul: Okay. Get on with it.

Some of the actors move a huge mirror into one corner of the stage. A few smaller looking glasses hang from the walls, the paraphernalia of a make-up room. The idea is to create a make-up room on the stage. The show opens the next day and the director wants to make a change now. The audience will hear what is going on in the make-up room. The actors will be wearing clothes from the Middle Ages. Rajat is wearing a choga and sitting on a stool in front of the mirror. He stares continuously at his face. He seems a bit lacking in self-confidence. As Dada darkens the area under his eyes, Rajat looks at him.

Dada: You have lost everything. You are totally defeated. When one is very sad, dark circles form under the eyes.

Rajat: (*His voice frightened*) Dada, I'll manage this, no?

Dada: Of course you will. You are an actor of darkness, of an interior darkness. You will pull this off, without a hitch.

He smudges the darkness under Rajat's eyes. As the first bell rings, Meena enters. She is in a terrible state.

Meena: I got late getting to school.

Rajat: How did you get late? Where is Angad?

Meena: He was not at the school gate when...

Mahendra: That's amazing, Bhabhi. How could you be so careless? If anything happens to Angad, I'll...

Shobha enters. Everyone looks at her with a mixture of terror and hope. The second bell.

Shobha: I got to the school and picked Angad up. He insisted that he wanted to go to the hospital to see the playwright. I want to sit with him and see the play.

Angad enters the hall, holding the playwright's hand. The playwright's wife holds his other hand. The third bell rings. Stage lights on. Make-up room in darkness. Mahendra is seen in a doorway in the garb of a messenger; Kanta in the other door. Rajat touches Dada's feet.

Mahendra: Rajan, today, your only begotten son...on the battle field.

Rajat turns to look at him. Then he turns to look at the audience. The spotlight follows him throughout his speech. Other lights low or completely out. The music follows the tonalities of the monologue.

Rajat: There was a boy whose legs... There was a boy who wanted to be an actor but he no longer had any legs. Because he did not live in our world where we are handicapped by possessing two legs. He had his own magical world. The one we call a stage. In this bewitching world, there is no inflation, no piles of corpses. This was where he could wash away the workaday world and its griefs, this world, the theatre. There was no bare-faced politicking here, the kind that breeds a society of the bloodthirsty and the bloodstained. But that boy died. There is special providence in the fall of a sparrow.

The dungeon of art, a dungeon on fire, pulsating with heat. Abandon the prospect of leaving, all those who enter here. There is no way out. No sunlight can enter, there is not a chink by which an errant ray might enter here. And yet we choose to enter this dungeon. Why do we choose to enter of our own free will? In the hope of mukti. For a personal mukti. To wash away our sorrow, agony, anger, violence, resentment and all that is misbegotten in us and all that stains our souls. To seek mukti for ourselves and for you. That is why we enter this world of illusion, the theatre. To free ourselves from the curse of being ourselves. (*Now his voice approaches delirium.*)

You too have probably been filled with rage by your children. And here, dressed in rags, screaming a challenge at the very elements, at the rain and the lightening, King Lear. We, we are Lear. And we are King Oedipus too, abandoning the topos of the body with its violations and betrayals, trembling at the extreme limits of a search for redemption, his eyes plucked out. We are Oedipus. We are Lord Rama, wandering in the forests. We are King Ravana, roaring in Lanka. We sit in this pulsating dungeon of fire, wiping away the wounds of every soul.

There was once a boy. He no longer had legs. And he wanted to be an actor. (*Repeat lines. A small silence, a pause. And now, in a calm voice:*)

May I tell you a tale from the Jataka? Lord Buddha was giving a sermon. No one can escape from the fruit of sin, from the fruit of one's karma. And then there came a mother, carrying her dead son in her arms, wailing her sorrow. This broken-hearted mother asked of the Enlightened One, 'What sin has my son committed in the short time he lived that he was given a death sentence? You are God. You can bring my son back to life.' Can even a God bear the sorrow of a bereaved mother? His eyes moist but with a gentle smile playing on his lips, Lord Buddha said, 'Go, mother, go bring me a pinch of ash from the hearth of a home that has known no death. Bring it to me and I will bring your son to life again. The mother was delighted. A pinch of ash? Just a pinch of ash to revive her son? Centuries passed. It is said that the mother is wandering from place to place, from house to house, looking for a home which has known no death. And through all the world, no one will give her this pinch of ash. (*The lights begin to dim*) There was once a boy. He had his own magical world. Which is known as the theatre. In this bewitching world, there is no inflation, no piles of corpses. But that boy died. There is special providence in the fall of a sparrow.

Curtain.

The Saddest Poem Ever Written

Translated by Jerry Pinto

Playwright's dedication:

For Nirmal Verma

~

Cast a cold eye.
On life, on death.
Horseman, pass by!

—W.B. Yeats

Cast

Apoorva: Journalist
Sukant: Doctor
Ramsharan: Compounder
Ahuja: DSP
Zamindar: Shivdayo Singh
Woman/Wife: The Zamindar's wife; unnamed
Jagmal Singh: Bodyguard
Suryaswami: Apoorva's colleague
Naren: Apoorva's colleague
Lakshman/SP: Superintendent of Police Lakshman
Daroga: Unnamed
Judge: Unnamed
Warder: Unnamed
Jailer: Unnamed

Act One

The last bell has rung. Darkness on a completely empty stage. Some actors read poetry in theatrical voices. By the time the poem ends, a dim light begins to illuminate the stage slowly.

She comes,
And from some corner of the earth
A lament arises.
From a corner of the sky,
ash begins to flow.

She comes
And tries to insert a comma
Into some sentence of life.

She sees yellow leaves falling
From green branches.

She comes,
But leaves no footprints
In the dust.
She has nothing to do with
our bodies.
She takes only our breath,
And takes it silently.
She can only be seen
by those to whom she comes.
The rest can only sense
That something has passed them by.

Scene 1

A small room in a very small hospital. Two chairs, one in front and one behind a table. A portion of the bench outside the room is visible. A single bulb casts a dirty light over the room. A young man enters the room, followed by a middle-aged man.

Ramsharan: Doctor Saahab. I need ten days' leave. My mother's illness is...

Dr Sukant: Have you ordered the bandages and medicine? I told you yesterday, Ramsharan.

Ramsharan: No funds, sir.

Sukant: The blood pressure machine isn't working. We have to...

Ramsharan: No funds, sir.

Sukant: I signed the cash book yesterday. We have some cash on hand.

Ramsharan: Sir, there's many a slip 'twixt yesterday and today. And if the Delhi government should slip...

Sukant: You don't worry about Delhi. Worry about the patients here. We have medicines.

A woman stands at the door, listening. She's well dressed with short hair hanging loose over her shoulders. A gentle smile plays on her lips. It is apparent that she is beautiful internally too.

Ramsharan: You've just come to this poor and backward place which is why you're so concerned. These people are in the habit of dying. They drink mahua and die. They drink home brew and die. They're caught with someone else's wife and are murdered. If they're spared your medicines, something or the other will definitely kill them. They fight each other. Or the zamindar's army will finish the job. But they are all fated to die at someone else's hands.

The woman enters the room. The middle-aged man bent over the table warns the doctor in his ear.

Ramsharan: Now watch your tongue. This is a journalist. Apoorva.

Apoorva: He's told you all, has he? But let's go through the formalities, anyway. I'm Apoorva, I work for the Delhi papers. Freelance. I know you from the nameplate outside. So, Dr Sukant, welcome to this godforsaken place.

Ramsharan: We didn't hear you come in. You have the footsteps of a spy...

Apoorva: Ramsharan, these days everyone has a spy following them. Government spies, our spies, or the spies of the soul. Do not train our new doctor to kill his patients. Or you'll have some people after your blood. Go get the medicines.

Ramsharan goes out, his gait revealing his fear. Sukant gestures Apoorva to a chair. When she sits down, he bows his head.

Apoorva: What brings you to this backward area? You must have brought your mother with you.

Sukant: My mother is dead.

Apoorva: Your father then...

Sukant: He's dead too.

Apoorva: Which means you'll never get married.

Sukant: Why? Why 'never'?

Apoorva: Because you don't seem able to look at a woman. Look how you're sitting now, your head bowed. As if you're afraid I'll cast the evil eye on you.

Sukant looks down a little more.

Apoorva: *Arre*, Dr Sukant, you're blushing. Such modesty! Such innocence! A Greek god but with the heart of a woman. So, tell me, how did you get such a beautiful and meaningful name? Who chose it?

Sukant: My mother.

Apoorva: She must have been well educated.

Sukant: No, but she was always reading poetry. I remember her with a book of poetry in her hands while my father would drink all day and night and sing Saigal songs in a terrifying voice.

Apoorva: (*Sadly*) A sad poem.

Sukant: Sorry, a what poem?

Apoorva: Yes, Dr Sukant. A woman is the saddest poem ever written. A worker who constantly fights and is constantly defeated is the saddest poem ever. A woman squatting in the fields to deliver a baby is the saddest poem. A chattering girl who stops talking suddenly is the saddest poem. When the last words of a dying man are finally forgotten, that is the saddest poem.

A short silence.

Sukant: I'm not sure I understand.

Apoorva: Yes, Dr Sukant. That which is true and that

which is right take time to understand. These people are stuck in quicksand. But they've begun to enjoy it. They will not come out to safe, firm ground. Do you know what they think? A flute-player will arrive one day and lead them to a heaven of happiness. Fools. Waiting for Godot.

Sukant: Godot? Who is Godot?

Apoorva: You haven't read it? But you seem to have read nothing other than your text books.

Sukant: Why do you say my name with so much irritation? Yes, I haven't read anything. My father died when I was doing my matric. I could continue to study because of his pension. I got good marks. Admission to medical college followed. When my mother died, the pension ended. I would take books from my seniors and make notes all night. Do you know what it's like to study when your stomach aches with hunger? No, you do not. You see the world with rose-coloured glasses. A bright, beautiful world of make-believe.

Apoorva: *Arre*, so you can be moved to anger too. Your mother read poetry, didn't she (*laughing delightedly*)? She must have named you for Sukant Bhattacharya, the warrior-poet.

Sukant: Who? Who is this Sukant Bhattacharya?

Apoorva: For those who know him, he is everything. For those who don't, nothing.

Sukant: You must lend me some good books to read, Apoorvaji.

Apoorva: Of course, Sukantji. But only if you drop the 'ji' you've tagged on to my name.

Sukant: I certainly will, Apoorva. But you must stop calling me Doctor. You say it as if it's a cuss word.

The compounder enters.

Ramsharan: The patients are here. If madam's interview is over, I might send them in? No rush. These people are used to sitting and waiting endlessly.

Sukant: Did you get the medicines from the chemist?

Ramsharan: Who knows you here? You've hardly been here a few days. Why would the chemist give me medicines on your say-so?

Sukant's head is bowed again. Apoorva turns her eyes on Ramsharan. Her gaze is stern.

Apoorva: Should I write a small news item? 'No medicines in dispensary despite cash available'. Oh, and let me give you some breaking news. In a few days, this habit of sitting and waiting...? It will end. And once they rise, they rise.

Ramsharan: No, madam. No need for news items and such. I'll bring the medicines in your name (*in a small voice*).

Sukant: You frightened him. He would have just back-answered me.

Apoorva: You do not wear a uniform.

Sukant: A uniform?

Apoorva: Yes. A white coat. In this country we are terribly scared of anyone who wears a uniform. A policeman can slap a dozen men or hit them with his shoes or beat them with his lathi, and people will stand by and watch. If a revolt happens and it grows, the government sends the army out on a flag march. We are not scared of people. We reserve our terror for those in power and their symbols: the uniforms.

Ramsharan enters. He puts the medicines on the table. He beckons the tea boy to come in. The boy sets a glass of tea down before each person.

Apoorva: You guessed his wishes before he expressed them. I was also dying for a cup of tea.

Ramsharan: Less sugar and strong. I know the way you like it.

Apoorva: Perhaps you know everything about me.

Ramsharan retreats, abashed, head bowed.

Sukant: Let's go out and see the patients. They've been waiting so long.

All three go out. On two benches, half-dressed men and women are sitting. Sukant starts examining them in order from the door, writes prescriptions which he puts in Ramsharan's hands, who doles out medicine. And then the sound of approaching footsteps. A man comes running in.

The Man: DSP Ahuja. Policemen with him. Ever since the zamindar's son has been killed, he's been after us, day and night. (*Turning to the women*) Go home all of you. And listen. If any man has not gone to work, send him here immediately.

He picks up the spear lying on the bench and takes up a position near Apoorva. The other two men pick up lathis. They form a protective cordon around her. The square their shoulders, their eyes are calm and unafraid. DSP Ahuja enters with two soldiers. His neck is stiff with pride. He walks with rapid steps up to the man who holds a spear and stares at him. The man stiffens his spine. Ahuja grabs the spear, takes it from him, flings it on the ground and pushes him backwards with a hand to his chest.

Ahuja: (*To his men*) Take their weapons from them. (*To the men forming the cordon*) Don't you know it's a crime to enter a government building with weapons? Next time, I'll arrest the lot of you.

The sepoys take the weapons out and return.

Apoorva: Those aren't weapons. In this state, they are a part of a person's body. As a sword is in your Punjab.

Ahuja: Hello, Miss Journalist. You know a lot about the Punjab, it seems.

Apoorva: We know a lot about the entire country, Mr DSP. I also know how powerful your political connections are. And as if you're running in fear from them, you've come to this state. A state of poor and powerless people, but a heaven for the police, a gold mine. You can kill anyone you want whenever you want in an encounter. And who in his right mind is going to complain?

Ahuja: (*Turning to the doctor*) How do you let such people come into your hospital? These people...

Sukant: Sorry, sir. I had no idea what kind of people...

Ahuja: A file has been opened on this woman. Come to the station whenever you want and look at it. We know everything about her.

Apoorva: We also know everything about you. In

Punjab, you killed three innocent people and tried to get the President's medal. They would not have spared your life, so you came running here on deputation. But they could follow you here too, for revenge is their dharma.

Ahuja: Don't shoot your mouth off. The day I get you in the station...

Apoorva: You'll gang rape me. As you did to that Adivasi woman. Your wife is so beautiful. Didn't she stink, that poor ugly woman? I hear you guys take great pleasure in raping defenceless women. It's as if your pride in your manhood grows by a few inches.

Ahuja: What do you know about my wife...?

Apoorva: She goes to the market alone. We know about your son, too. He is in the third standard in the Carmel Convent. Two of your men escort him to school. Until school lets out, they sit at the gate, smoking beedis. We have a file on you as well.

Ahuja: What have my wife and son ever...

Apoorva: Nothing. Nothing at all, DSP Saahab. But war has been declared, and in a war, good strategy demands that one know one's enemy.

Ahuja: Don't threaten me. I can put you behind bars...

Apoorva: Those days are gone when you could arrest people and murder them.

Ahuja: (*Sarcastically*) What days?

Apoorva: Old sins have long shadows.

Ahuja: (*Startled*) What?

Apoorva: Old sins have long shadows, and in those shadows, the wind has turned cold and cruel. Now the very air will mount an attack.

Ahuja: I would not raise my hand to a woman for fear of God. Or else...

Apoorva: Do not fear God. Why should you fear God? Fear your fellow man. There is rage in the eyes of people. They now think differently and this is rewriting their souls. Everything rotten will be burned to the roots.

Ahuja: Don't go all fancy on me. I know you went to a convent school. I know you've been in this area for the last two years. You have the excuse of being a journalist so you instigate people, you stir them up. And I also know you keep all the fugitives informed. I know you killed the zamindar's son. I know...

Apoorva: If you know all this, why haven't you arrested me?

Ahuja: I will. You bet I will. When I get proof, then it will be you and me, face to face.

Apoorva: That will be a terrible day.

Ahuja: Really? Why?

Apoorva: Beware the dark shadows cast by old sins.

Ahuja: (*To the half-clad men*) If I see you again with weapons... (*To Sukant*) Doctor, this woman should not come here again. Or I will suspend you. (*To Apoorva*) Goodbye, Miss Journalist. We will meet soon—the final meeting between law and anarchy.

Apoorva: Goodbye, Mr DSP. We will indeed meet soon. Between the air gone mad and the helpless straw.

Exit Ahuja and men. The men guarding her come closer to Apoorva.

The Man: Didi, should we just finish him...?

Apoorva: No. Let his atrocities increase. Then we will kill him. And the people will celebrate his death with a festival.

She goes to Sukant.

Apoorva: The police frighten you.

Sukant: Yes.

Apoorva: You must become dangerous too.

Sukant: What? Become what?

Apoorva: Dangerous.

Sukant: Why?

Apoorva: Because people are frightened of dangerous men.

Sukant: True. But how can I?

Apoorva: We'll make you forbidding. (*She smiles*) Okay. I'm going now.

Sukant: When will you come, Apoorvaji?

Apoorva: How much you fear! Call me Apoorva.

Sukant: (*Ducking his head*) You will come, won't you, Apoorva?

Apoorva: I will. Of course I will come, my fraidy-cat Greek god.

The tinkling of anklets is heard.

Darkness.

Scene 2

In a large, well-appointed sitting room sits a grand middle-aged man. In his hand, he holds a Hindi book. His armed bodyguard appears at the door.

The Zamindar: Come in. Come in Jagmal Singh. Has someone come to see...

Jagmal: Yes, sir. (*With dislike*) That police chap. DSP Ahuja. And up to now the young master's murder remains...

Zamindar: He will not be able to apprehend them. We will have to pick up our weapons soon. But let him keep trying for a few more days. The more he fails, the further he will fall in his own eyes. When his self-confidence is crushed, he will crawl to us, asking for help. And then he will be a toy in our hands. Send him in.

Jagmal goes to the door. He turns to look at the Zamindar.

Zamindar: Do you want to say something? Go on. Say it without fear.

Jagmal: The sparks are beginning to dance in my palms.

Zamindar: So, it is time to kill someone? The river is on fire. Stop. Hold on. Hold on for a few more days. Let our strategy come to fruit. (*Jagmal turns to leave.*) When Ahuja comes in, go out and see whether his car is old or new. Then come and tell me in my ear.

Jagmal looks perplexed. He goes out. Ahuja is at the door. He stops there.

Zamindar: Why have you stopped, Ahuja? Come in. Sit by my side.

Ahuja: Would that I were deserving of such an honour for I...

Zamindar: Do not use that courtier-like language with me. I am not your senior officer. So why use the language of the castrated? The men of your area are powerful but when they are confronted with their elders and betters, they meow like kittens.

Ahuja: Yes, zamindar saahab. You're completely correct in your analysis...

Zamindar: Friends do not 'analyse', Ahuja; they say things. But it is not your fault. Those who are close to power and live in the shadow of the ruler will always end up powerless, unable to think. It is as if termites consume their ability to think. You have always been close to Delhi. First the Mughals, then the British and now the little foxes of our political leaders. How would you develop self-confidence or the desire to make decisions? Never mind. Nothing will come of this talk. (*In a harsh voice*) At what stage is the investigation into my son's death?

Ahuja: No clues have emerged and no evidence has come to light to lead us to the murderer.

Zamindar: Do not use the singular. *Murderers*, not murderer. In our entire state, is there a man who could single-handedly kill my son? These revolutionaries surrounded him and killed him. There were dozens of murderers.

Ahuja: Yes, indeed, sir. There was a crowd that surrounded him. But we need to identify the one who killed him and collect evidence against...

Zamindar: You won't be able to identify anyone. You will not find any evidence. These guerrilla fighters never leave any traces behind. They are committed to their cause. They want political change through armed revolution.

Ahuja: I heard that the young master was very kind-hearted...

Zamindar: He was. And that was his fault. I sent him abroad to study. He became modern. I sent a warrior son and I got a bleeding heart back. He immediately gave in to the demands of the workers. From one kilo of rice to one-and-a-half. Houses near the fields. When they tasted a little happiness, it only increased their aspirations for more. Compassion makes us lame tigers who can no longer leap on their prey. He forgot that for us compassion must be staged as theatre is staged. A few scraps of sympathy should be tossed to them from time to time. When hundreds of people die in a disaster, what do the Prime Minister and President do? They send a message of condolence. Does a ruler ever give his life for them?

A dignified woman enters. Behind her a servant, ghoonghat covering her head, a tea tray in her hands.

Ahuja: (*Gets up, goes to her, bows*) *Pranaam mataji*, I am...

Woman: Sit down where you were. How did you find the courage to address me as your mother? My young son was murdered, and you will insult me by addressing me as mother? To what end? To drive another nail into my heart?

Zamindar: Why did you come here? Go rest in your...

Woman: Yes, indeed I should rest. That is all I do. I rest and in my rest, I am supposed to forget my son's murder and all the rest of it.

Ahuja: Be patient. The murderers of the young master will...

Woman: When a prince dies, a hundred others must die in redress.

When beggars die, there are no comets seen;
The heavens themselves blaze forth the death of princes.

Ahuja looks at her surprised.

Woman: You haven't read Shakespeare, then? You should. Julius Caesar. Act II, Scene 2.

Zamindar: Calm yourself. I will talk to him.

Woman: How am I to calm myself? My son is murdered and I must be calm? The murderers wander at will and I must be calm? What sort of father are you? Will you turn your son's murder into a political tool? We are of royal blood, descended from kings. We have not the habit of wandering down these contorted roads. We walk the royal road, the high road. Having dealt so long with politicians, has your heart weakened? We know how to use guns. We have our own army. At any moment, we will witness the embodiment of Ranchandi Mata.

Ahuja: We have found out that the young master was killed on the directions of that journalist Apoorva. Perhaps that young woman and he were...

Woman: Yes. He liked her. What surprise in that? Women have always been sex objects for warriors and governors. Vasundhara was consumed by warriors. And was not Draupadi the wife of the five Pandavas? Then another hundred wanted to have her. And the Mahabharata began.

Ahuja: Any day now, I'll deal with her in an encounter...

Woman: No, do not kill her in an encounter. Find the evidence you need and create the perfect case. She should receive a life sentence. I want to see her die every day. I want her death to last a lifetime.

Jagmal enters, gives the Zamindar something. The serving woman serves tea.

Zamindar: (*Pushes some car keys over to Ahuja*) Here, a new car. Go and get it from our showroom tomorrow. A brave officer like you should not drive an old car like that. Leave your old car behind at the showroom. The manager will give you a reasonable price.

Ahuja: No, sir. Don't embarrass me. When the work is done, maybe...

Woman: You will have to do the work, whether you take the car or not. What a happy family you have. Never, even for a moment, should we doubt your loyalty. That would mean the apocalypse for you...

Ahuja: Your wish is my command. Just tell me...what you want me to do...

Woman: You have to do nothing. Any evening now, bullets will fly. On that evening the police will stay at home for as long as the bullets fly. Now you will show your face here only after that evening of the flying bullets. He has given you a car, I will give you a house. (*She begins to leave*) Now we cry havoc and let slip the dogs of war. Now a thousand men must bleed to stanch the wounds of my son. How sweet is the smell of spilt enemy blood!

Ahuja: I will do as I am told. But if there's action taken against me...

Zamindar: There will be. You will be suspended. In a month we will get you out. We will have to throw some dust in the eyes of the people and the media.

Ahuja: (*Stands up*) Very well, sir. Will you please let me know first...

Zamindar: You will know when the rest of the country finds out. Murder is not committed with due warning. Now go. Go straight home. (*His voice is harsh*) Your wife may worry.

Exit Ahuja. Zamindar beckons Jagmal to him.

Zamindar: Keep a constant watch on him. He is a coward and may well be a traitor. If he ever seems to be on his way to meet the Inspector-General or the Deputy Inspector-General, kill him. Kill him in public. And the flames dancing on your palms will be quenched.

Jagmal goes to the door, unconsciously rubbing his palms together.

Zamindar: One moment, come here.

Jagmal: (*Approaches*) Yes, bade sarkar.

Zamindar: That journalist, Apoorva.

Jagmal: That I cannot do, sarkar. Not the murder of a woman.

Zamindar: Do not interrupt. I know you will not murder women or children. Go and warn Apoorva of Ahuja's intentions.

Jagmal: Sarkar, I don't understand...

Zamindar: You do not have to understand everything. Two enemies turn to confront each other; that is part of strategy. Go to Apoorva and...

Jagmal now rubs his palms constantly. To the tune of ghunghroos and terrifying nagaada drums.

Darkness.

Scene 3

Sukant and a young man at the door. Half the stage in darkness.

Sukant: How was Apoorva hurt?

Naren: I told you. A wild animal wandered into the fields. Apoorva fired at it with a country-made revolver. The barrel burst.

Sukant: You must think me a complete fool. Apoorva? At night? In the fields?

Naren: Who said it was night? These days wild animals

prowl by day. On the highways and the byways. The man-hunting animals of India are on the rampage.

Sukant: Apoorva was guarding the fields? Why? Tell me the truth. You should have brought her to the hospital.

Naren: Please, Dr Sukant. No discussions please. I am just the messenger. Asking too many questions can be dangerous sometimes.

Sukant: Why is it always threats...?

Naren: It's only that language that the so-called well-born class understands.

They move to the dark half of the stage. It lights up. On a chair, a pillow. Her eyes closed, Apoorva sprawls in it. When they approach, her eyes open. A gentle smile.

Sukant: (*Goes to Apoorva*) I thought it was the sun, resting on a pillow.

Apoorva: Sukant *re* Sukant. He's turned into a poet, has our Sukant.

She tries to clap. The hurt hand sends out a sunburst of pain. She uses the other hand to stifle a cry. Sukant moves her hand from her face and holds it. She smiles.

Sukant: So much pain and still you're smiling.

Apoorva: To smile when in pain is a habit with us. We've wept too many tears in search of a little compassionate alms-giving.

Sukant: Who tied this bandage...?

Naren: I did. And gave her pain killers.

Sukant: Since when did you become a doctor?

Naren: Ever since we decided to fight our own battles we have rejected all middlemen. We bind up our own wounds now.

Sukant: (*Sadly*) Yes. You lot know it all. Everything. What you do not know is the language of explanation, of ordinary conversation.

Apoorva: The weapons of conversation have changed. For fifty years we listened to shining lies. Now we choose the weapons that suit the fight.

Sukant: Which fight are you talking about? The one in which you kill a few people and then get killed as a result? This is a suicidal fight. But the way of compromise...

Naren: Nothing will be achieved by talking about compromise. It is one of those mantras dear to the ruling class—keep the velvet glove over the iron fist. In every fight, some people are destined to die. Sometimes it is one of us, sometimes one of the enemy. Those who believe in armed revolution cannot fear the spilling of blood.

Sukant: Let's get Apoorva to hospital.

Apoorva: No. You must do what you have to here. The hospital is being watched by Ahuja's men. Any one of our wounded taken there will be arrested. And perhaps you too.

Seeing his worried face, she laughs uproariously.

Sukant: Stop laughing, will you?

Apoorva: Our Sukant is getting angry. The first sign of impending manhood.

Sukant: I do not want to become a man who goes around murdering.

Naren: Don't call it murder. In a political war, it is assassination. And this is an assassination committed by thought, not by hand or weapon.

Sukant opens his medical bag. Enter Jagmal Singh, walking with quick steps. He has a sword in his hand. Naren and Apoorva's faces reflect their fear. Naren jumps for his bag which is at a distance from him.

Jagmal: No, babu saahab. No need for weapons. I don't have permission to kill you yet. Not from Bade Saahab and not from Mahakaal.

Sukant: Who is this?

Naren: Bade Sarkar's hired killer.

Jagmal: No, babu saahab. I do not kill on Bade Sarkar's orders because I get paid. I just happen to like taking life. When my palms begin to burn, I have to kill. (*Shouldering his spear, he begins to rub his palms together.*) Those flames again. Now whose life must I take?

Apoorva: Enough of this talk about murder. You kill, so do we. It's on, our blood-soaked war. Someone or the other will have to die. (*She smiles*) So tell me. Why are you here? Do you have a message for me?

Jagmal: No, Didi. The likes of Bade Sarkar do not send messages. I have a message of ceasefire. Be careful of that Ahuja. He has accepted huge sums of money for your life.

Naren: There must be some reason for this warning, some dire agenda. Hired killers rarely feel sympathy for...

Jagmal: You're right, saahab. But then you have no trust in God and not in fate either. So what is the point in telling you? But still I am here to warn you. I was born to kill, but to kill men. The day I kill a woman or a child, my strength will be taken from me. And saahab, imagine what use a cowardly and weak warrior would be. So beware of that DSP. If he finds out that she has been wounded, you will see how he will turn it into an encounter killing.

In the doorway, Ahuja with his men.

Ahuja: Ahuja has found out. (*He plants himself in front of Apoorva.*) Madam Journalist, your time is up. Who did you shoot? Whose bullet hurt your hand?

He pulls her out of her chair by her wounded hand. Apoorva lets loose a tiny scream. Sukant moves forward and grabs Ahuja's hand; Ahuja shoves him aside.

Sukant: You cannot treat my patient like that. Grabbing her by her wounded hand... I will file a report of police torture.

Ahuja: Where did you find the courage to open your mouth in front of me?

Apoorva: You don't have to find courage. It's inside us. It comes from the wind hiding in the trees. From the tiger, crouched in the shade; from the blood running in our veins; from the words of great men—sometimes it takes us time to recognize it. But then the breeze whispers in one's ear: wake up, rise. The labour pains of a woman giving birth in the fields say to us: Wake up, rise. And the smoke, acrid and black, from the factories, says: Wake up, rise. The lost giggles of children remind us: Wake up, rise. The poetry of

Nirala says: Wake up, rise. And when we find our strength, the singing of Kumar Gandharva announces: They have risen.

She falls back into her chair, out of breath. She strokes the wounded hand with the other one. Sukant proffers medicines. Jagmal fetches a glass of water from outside. He puts it into her hand and then, bowing, touches her feet.

Jagmal: You are an avatar, Maa. An avatar of Mahakaal.

Ahuja: (*Beckons Jagmal with his index finger*) Come here.

Jagmal: (*In front of him*) Saahab, in this state, that is how we call dogs.

Ahuja: I have seen you somewhere. Where?

Jagmal: In Bade Sarkar's haveli, saahab.

Ahuja: You are his hired gunman. What do they call it here? A mukhbir.

Jagmal: I don't know the Hindi word for 'hired gunman'. I do know a little English. After all, I did fail high school... You didn't ask why I failed high school.

Ahuja: (*Contemptuously*) Tell me, then.

Jagmal: High school. The history teacher, a mine of cusswords. One day he used filthy words for my mother. I killed him. In front of the whole school.

Ahuja: How did you escape?

Jagmal: I was taken under Bade Sarkar's protection. He told the headmaster to change my date of birth in the school register. I went from being an adult to being underage. Even five thousand rupees was not enough. That's when Bade Sarkar revealed what the pandit said.

Ahuja: What pandit? What did he say?

Jagmal: Saahab, when I was a child my mother took me to a learned pandit. He refused to say anything after looking at my hand. My mother insisted and finally he told her what he had seen.

Ahuja: And which was?

Jagmal: That I would kill twenty-five people. Hearing this, my mother fainted.

Ahuja steps back two paces.

Jagmal: Up to now I have killed twenty-one people. Each time I have been caught. Each time I have been let go too. No one gives evidence against me. But I only kill men. Never women or children.

Ahuja: So, the zamindar sent you...

Jagmal: (*Goes on, unheeding*) Now four more people must die by my hand. When it is time to kill someone, my palms begin to burn.

The spear goes back on his shoulder. He begins to rub his palms again. Apoorva gets out of her chair, faces Ahuja.

Apoorva: Why did the zamindar send Jagmal here?

Ahuja: How would I know? Ask him (*pointing to Jagmal*).

Apoorva: Ahuja, you know why. You are in league with the zamindar.

Ahuja: Do not speak to the police like that. You are a woman. The fear of God stays my hand or...

Apoorva: Do not fear God. Fear women. If anything happens today...

Enter a wounded youth.

Wounded youth: The zamindar's army has attacked...

Apoorva: How many dead?

Wounded youth: Sixty. Women and children too.

Apoorva: The police?

Wounded youth: No one came. The daroga is on holiday. And the DSP...

Apoorva: ...is here. To enact the drama of my arrest.

Ahuja: We understand guerrilla tactics too.

Apoorva: But you have never fought a straightforward war. A war to light a fire in the blood. This is the war we will now fight, Ahuja. For half a kilo of rice you let sixty die.

Ahuja: Half a kilo of rice?

Apoorva: Yes. Half a kilo of rice. What were the demands of the landless workers? That they be paid two kilos instead of one-and-a-half kilo. For half a kilo of rice you let sixty bonded labourers die. What kind of womb did you spring from?

Ahuja: (*Angry*) Don't you dare abuse my mother.

Apoorva: All the world will abuse her. (*She grabs his collar*) Oh, you'll get your bravery award, all right. But posthumously. (*In a cold, hard voice*) I, Apoorva, hereby sentence you to death, you mad dog. I, Apoorva, award you the death sentence. You shall die by burning, for murdering sixty people for only half a kilo of rice.

Freeze. The sharp, frightening sounds of anklets and nagaada drums.

Darkness.

Act Two

Scene 1

A small room. A stuffed book rack. Chairs around the table. A surahi in a corner. Apoorva is writing something. Enter Sukant.

Sukant: This room is very small.

Apoorva: (*Smiles*) After we marry, we'll get a bigger room...

Sukant: (*Annoyed with her*) Why do you always tease?

Apoorva: Why do you always get angry? I will spend my life, it seems, trying to calm you down. Okay, let me try. I enjoy cajoling you out of a bad temper. Will you have tea? I make a good cup of tea.

Sukant: Girls who murder people don't make good tea.

Apoorva: And who have I killed? It seems you're spoiling for a fight.

Sukant: These sixty people who died. Sixty post-mortems...

Apoorva: No one will require you to perform post-mortems. When many poor people die, the government waives post-mortems. One more way to pacify the poor.

Sukant: But those people did get killed. I've been with the civil surgeon to the village. It's all silent. Everywhere, silence. In the lanes, in the houses. On the faces of people. Death still crouches among them.

Apoorva: In a war, some people are destined to die.

Sukant: (*Angry*) Now you get to make decisions about who lives and who dies. When did you become God?

Apoorva: (*Hard*) No. God does not make decisions about life and death. This is something put about by the priests and the ruling class. It's a myth. More than ninety per cent of the people live below the poverty line. Each day they die by inches. It's a slow but sure death. Which God decided that they would die in this way?

Sukant: But...

Apoorva: But nothing. If you believe in armed revolution, you do not cry over the fallen. You look for other ways to kill the enemy. You cannot afford the luxury of sentiment. Do you expect us to turn away from the road we have chosen? No. Nothing is given to the poor on a platter. They have to fight, they have to kill.

Sukant: You people talk in a manner that is almost as frightening as your actions. (*He takes her wounded hand*) Here, let me change your bandage.

Apoorva: (*Smiles*) Nothing is the matter with it. You keep looking at my hand. Sometimes, look at me as well.

Sukant: (*Looking into her eyes*) Apoorva, I...

Apoorva: No, don't say that word. The moment it is spoken, the moment it is heard, we will be cursed. We have no time for that word. The river has just broken from the mountains. That word will make it forget to flow. It is a word with great power. It could stop us. It could take us right back to where we began.

Sukant: 'So fair was never so fatal'.

Apoorva: You've begun reading the books I gave you. Now you have become intelligent.

Sukant: I don't know whether I'm intelligent or cowardly. When you forbid me to use a word to you...

Apoorva: Can you admit me to your hospital for two days? Starting this morning.

Sukant: Yes, there are two beds. In an emergency, we can...

Apoorva: Then do it. I am your emergency patient.

Sukant: Your hand is getting better...

Apoorva: You worry too much, Sukantji. If you want to save me from the police then admit me to the hospital. Or the next time we meet will be in the police station or in jail.

Sukant: (*Unblinking*) You threatened to murder the DSP. Is that why...

Apoorva: It was not a threat, it was a sentence that I passed.

Sukant: Who are you to pass a sentence on him? Are you a judge?

Apoorva: If a judge can accept a fat salary to listen to false witnesses and hand down sentences, why can't I? Dr Sukant, they make judgements; we do justice in the courts of the people.

Sukant: Justice is also offered by the system...

Apoorva: It is not. We are not talking about systems here but about a way of thinking, a point of view. People are now in the habit of seeing nothing. To catch the murderer of the zamindar's son, DSP Ahuja stripped the clothes of twenty women. He dragged them to the marketplace naked. Think about it. Twenty naked women walking through a public place. The stark naked women of India.

People could not bear the sight. They lowered their eyes, they turned away. It takes a great deal of shameless courage to look at a woman naked in public. Who knows whether on the occasion of this great victory he made the women sing 'Vande Mataram' or not. This is the golden jubilee of our stripping women.

Sukant: But...

Apoorva: People have grown accustomed to leading lives of indignity. Those in power will make your self-respect their first target. And this ends the power to stand in opposition.

Sukant: And what will a few armed people do...?

Apoorva: We are addicted to dreaming. But dreaming with eyes wide open is dangerous.

Sukant: But people die...

Apoorva: Death is liberation. We do not have an impure desire to rule. We do not wish to commit political sins.

Sukant: (*Sadly*) Apoorva, if something happens to you...

Apoorva: It will happen. Death. I will be killed in a police encounter. Or I will die at the hands of the government. At the end of a rope.

Sukant: What will I do then? You know what you are to me...

Apoorva: I know. *Arre*, I know you like me. Why do

you say it with such fear? Since when is it a bad thing to like someone? Oh, Sukant. My dear Sukant. My poor Sukant. I tremble to think of you living among your enemies. (*Angrily*) You fool. You bloody big fool. Why are you living in such an innocent world?

The sad sound of anklets fades into silence.

Sukant: Apoorva, are you angry...?

Apoorva: No. I'm not angry. I have not the good fortune to be angry with you.

Sukant: (*In a lost voice*) What will I do then? What will happen when you are not...?

Apoorva: Then who will babble at you? There'll be no one to answer your half questions with long tirades. The rivers will stop running. The caves will deepen, they will darken. The winds may stop from time to time to ask after you. You will lose your way in the jungle and there will be no one to take your hand and lead you back. And slowly you will begin to forget, even the last word of my last sentence will slip away from you. Sukant, oh, Sukant. My innocent fool.

Sukant puts his hand on hers. For a few moments, the sweet tinkle of ghungroos. Naren comes in with three young men. Apoorva and Sukant stand up. The four youths will keep some distance between each other. The spotlight will hit the person speaking.

Youth 1: DSP Ahuja is dead.

Naren: He was killed just as decided. His jeep was standing in the middle of the bazaar. Four constables were nearby.

Ahuja's eyes were sweeping the crowd; he was seated like a raja surveying his kingdom. We got to the jeep. Reading the words of the death sentence that was blazoned on our foreheads, the constables fled. We tied him with a rope to his seat.

Youth 2: The people stood off a little. They were silent spectators. There was no fear in their eyes, only pride. It took only four boys to deal with the man who paraded women naked.

Youth 3: Ahuja began to cry. He began to remember all the helpless victims he had killed, sometimes through encounters, sometimes in the fields and sometimes at the police station.

Naren: One can of petrol. Just one can. It was enough to take revenge. For all the honour of those naked women. One match stick. He burned, his jeep burned as Holika burns. We ran. Some people were applauding. Some were dancing.

Apoorva: Congratulations. All four of you, congratulations. Go on now, leave for Andhra. Do not use the trains. Take any truck. The entire state machinery will have been driven mad by this.

Youth 1: And those sixty people who were murdered?

Apoorva: The condolences of the President and the Prime Minister have been printed. The Chief Minister has asked the army and the Border Security Force to help. He felt so bad he had to air-dash to Delhi.

Naren: And the opposition parties...?

Apoorva: They are asking the Chief Minister to resign. This is not the time to take up arms. If they come to power those very weapons might be used against them. Their version of democracy cannot run without these murderers.

Ramsharan comes running in, out of breath.

Ramsharan: The police are going to raid us. They're on their way. Madam, you should apply for anticipatory bail.

Apoorva: Your network is very powerful, Ramsharanji. People like us do not apply for anticipatory bail.

Ramsharan: The poor find out the bad news first. (*To Sukant*) You should run, Doctor Saahab. You'll be arrested on suspicion.

Sukant: No. Now I won't run. I've run enough.

Apoorva: (*To the youths*) Go. Now.

Ramsharan: (*His voice close to tears*) But why don't you go with them. In the police station, they will... You will...

Apoorva: They'll rape me? Let them catch me. It is important for someone to be arrested. Or else hundreds will be arrested. It is time. This is my time to be arrested.

A silence followed by terrifying music played with ghungroos and nagaadas. The policemen come in.

Daroga: Come with us, the Superintendent of Police has called you.

Apoorva: (*Smiles*) Let's go, Daroga Saahab. I'll get a chance to meet your SP. I've heard so much about him.

The nagaada plays.

Darkness.

Scene 2

SP Lakshman is in mufti. He has a gentle personality. He speaks softly. In front of the table in his office, two chairs. Enter Daroga with Apoorva and Sukant.

Daroga: Sir...

SP: (*Gesturing to Sukant*) And who is this?

Daroga: Dr Sukant, sir. About a year ago he came to the dispensary here.

SP: He was not called.

Daroga: I tried to stop him, sir. I tried my best. But he insisted on coming.

SP: Dr Sukant, please sit outside.

Sukant: No, sir. I will stay with Apoorva.

SP: And why will you stay with Apoorva? Are you her guardian? She is an adult, is she not?

Sukant: I am going to marry her, I am her fiancé.

For a few moments, both the SP and Apoorva look at him astonished.

SP: Congrats, Dr Sukant. What a pair. What a combination. A healer and a killer. Sit down. Both of you.

They sit.

SP: You are Apoorva, the journalist.

Apoorva: (*Smiles*) Apoorva the killer. As you said just now.

SP: You are under arrest for...

Apoorva: Sir, you speak English well.

SP: Why do you think of the IAS and the IPS as illiterate? I know ten languages. And in each of those languages, the sentence for murder is the noose.

Apoorva: Okay, sir. You know ten languages. Congratulations. But do you understand any of them? You all know the language of the stick, the language of rape, the language of atrocity, and the ultimate language of encounter. Which one will you use on me?

SP: We will use the language of the land (*smiling*). Three days in police remand.

Sukant: She has been in hospital since yesterday. What proof is there?

SP: Doctor Saahab, when the police take you into remand, proof follows on its own. Evidence and witnesses too.

Apoorva: We have witnesses as well. They will tell you that I never left the room.

SP: People came inside though. Those four who poured petrol and burned Ahuja alive. What had they come for?

Apoorva: I'm a journalist. My job requires me to meet all kinds of people. And what proof do you have that they were the one who poured the petrol? Like hundreds of others, they too were watching a mad dog die.

SP: Do you think I will lose my temper like that fool Ahuja? Wrong. I taught communism for three years in the police training college.

Apoorva: No, sir. You taught how to exterminate communism for three years.

SP: A handful of armed revolutionaries can do nothing, can change nothing.

Apoorva: When the roots are rotten, you cannot save the branches. And when a part of the body rots, it must be amputated. Dire diseases need dire remedies.

SP: What good did the Naxalite movement in Bengal do?

Apoorva: The scent spread across the nation, the scent of the blood of oppressors. And across the country some people grew a few inches. Across the country, many people began to understand that only the sacrifice of life will bring the winds of change. Across the country, people learned that you do not get your rights by picking up a begging bowl but by reaching for a gun, that power flows through the barrel of a gun.

SP: I have read Mao and Marx and taught them too. I know the tactics and strategies of guerrilla warfare. You are the leader of the conspiracy to murder Ahuja. Four others were involved but yours was the brain behind it all.

Apoorva: Not four. A hundred thousand people killed him.

SP: A hundred thousand. Have you gone mad?

Apoorva: Yes, sir. A hundred thousand. Those people in front of whom he paraded twenty women naked over two kilometres... Those people who knew he was a silent spectator to the murder of sixty men, women and children. Those people whose support gave the boys their courage to carry out the sentence passed on Ahuja.

Daroga grabs her by the shoulder, shakes her.

Daroga: How dare you talk to the SP like that? I'm going to...

SP: Inspector. How dare you touch her at all? This is not your police station. This is my office. Do you understand?

Daroga backs off, head bowed.

SP: (*To Apoorva*) Do you think social change will come if you kill one police officer?

Apoorva: One death will lead to another death. It will free the people from terror.

SP: You call murder and bloodshed revolution?

Apoorva: We call it a path to peace. A peace between equals. Peace emerging from within. Not a peace imposed by the police and the army.

SP: You're right. And what of those who killed those sixty people?

Apoorva: They will be killed too. You even know who they were. You know who the leader of that army was. But you will neither capture them nor kill them because your political masters have not given you the orders. But they will die. The people will kill them. When the soul awakens...

SP: But I thought you people did not believe in things like the soul.

Apoorva: The strategies have changed, sir. We now talk in the language of the people.

SP: You have made an application for bail.

Apoorva: How do you expect to win this case if you have no proof?

SP: Who told you the police will make its case in court? Not now, Apoorva, not yet. But I do know this. You will die at my hands. When I make my case you will go straight from the courtroom to death row. It will be an air-tight case. No court in the world would set you free. I have already had seven people hanged. May God save you from my hands.

Sukant: You will not be able to hold her.

SP: And why not, Doctor Saahab? Read a few law books too. The police has the right to arrest someone on suspicion to investigate. Let me give you some advice. You might lose your job over this Apoorva.

Sukant: I know, sir. My life too.

SP: Love makes us bold and reckless. (*To the Daroga*) Take Apoorva away. Put some lady policewomen on duty. Beware. When a journalist is arrested, all the newspapers in the country will make a hue and cry about it. A special breed created by the Almighty.

Sukant: Her hand is wounded. She is under my treatment.

SP: There's nothing wrong with her hand. You doctors always work against the police.

Sukant: Sir, now you are talking nonsense. Are you a doctor or am I? Do you have an MBBS or an MD or do I?

SP: Cool down, my brave doctor, cool down. The civil surgeon will make that decision. (*To the Daroga*) Go. And call the civil surgeon. Tell him I have asked him to come. Take the jeep. (*The Daroga goes. To Sukant and Apoorva*) You two, wait outside.

The light dims. Sukant stands, his head bowed, some distance from Apoorva. Apoorva goes to him and touches him gently on the head. She smiles. Sukant smiles too. Apoorva takes his hand. They begin to walk together. We hear the sweet tinkling of ghunghroos.

Darkness.

Scene 3

In a large room, a grand old man, a book in hand. His wife sits in front of him. We hear the sweet sounds of ghungroos.

Wife: What are you reading?

Husband: *Urvashi* by Dinkarji.*

Wife: Is this the time to read about Urvashi? Read 'Ram ki Shakti Puja' by Niralaji. Your chest will expand and grow to pachydermal proportions. I haven't seen Jagmal Singh all day. Have you sent...

Husband: Today he has gone to save someone, not to kill.

Wife: Who?

Husband: He has gone to warn Apoorva. To beware of Ahuja.

Wife: Do you know what are you saying? Will you save your son's killer? Are you sure you haven't fallen prey to her deadly charms in the way your son did?

---

* *Urvashi* by Dinkarji is a long poem based on the love story of the apsara Urvashi and the earthly king Puruvara. Dinkarji won the Gyanpith award for this.

Husband: Why must you always talk of anger? Wars are not won with anger. Have you forgotten the efficacy of sweet poisons? Let the DSP and Apoorva fight each other. Let them kill each other.

At the door, a servant, her head bowed.

Wife: What is it?

Servant: That policeman who came here a few days ago?

Husband: DSP Ahuja. Does he want to meet me?

Servant: No, Bade Sarkar. It will not be possible to meet him in this life. He was murdered in the middle of the street.

Wife: Who killed him? How?

Servant: Some young men. They tied him up in his car, poured petrol on him and burned him alive.

Wife: Who were they?

Servant: Hundreds saw them. No one saved him and no one identified the young men.

Wife: Good. That is perfect. This is good news. You may take two kilos of rice from the store. Go.

Exit the servant.

Husband: One person less who knew the secret of the sixty murders. Now for the journalist Apoorva.

Wife: Do not use her name. Never in my presence. She is not a woman, she is a succubus, a woman who drinks blood.

Husband: And yet your son loved...

Wife: That was his mistake. Royalty is not supposed to fall in love. We simply use people. Read your history. A king always had dozens of queens. Could he have loved them all?

No. After he'd used them, they simply became one more ornament in his palace.

Husband: How do I fit in with all this? Don't compare me to...

Wife: (*Smiles*) You turned out to be different. Our marriage had been fixed. I was sent to England to study. But that didn't stop you. How many times you came to meet me. And in secret too.

Husband: I thought you might fall for a lord or a duke.

Wife: Oh you! You could have stopped me from going with a single message to my father. But my luck was to find a brave and wise man.

Enter Jagmal Singh, his sword in hand.

Bade Sarkar: Come in, Jagmal. Tell me, what news? Have you met that journalist?

Jagmal Singh comes in. His body shows his jitteriness. His sword seems stuck to his shoulder. He begins to rub his palms.

Jagmal: Yes, Bade Sarkar. I did warn her about Ahuja.

Bade Sarkar: They killed Ahuja. Burned him alive. You will have to give them that: these people take action swiftly. They murdered him in broad daylight. They made just one mistake: hundreds of witnesses who watched him burn alive.

Jagmal: It was no mistake. They thought this through carefully. They do not hide and kill as we do. They did it this way in order to reduce the fear people have of the police and the government. I have killed twenty-one people in front of everyone. And that is why they fear me.

Bade Sarkar: You were late returning.

Jagmal: Yes. I came by the fields. I went to see the massacre. I went to see how many had been killed on behalf of the young master. (*To the Zamindar*) Bade Sarkar, why did you not tell me? Why did you not send me? Did you think I would be a coward and...

Bade Sarkar: Do not talk like that. You, a coward? If I fear anyone, it is you. When you decide to take someone's life you will. But...

Jagmal: (*Rubbing his palms*) But what, Bade Sarkar?

Bade Sarkar: I know you to be half a warrior. You will not kill women and children. Well then...

We begin to hear the sound of ghungroos and nagaadas. The wife sees Jagmal rubbing his palms quicker and quicker. She gets up and leaves the room with quick steps.

Jagmal: How many were killed, sarkar?

Bade Sarkar: I am not a teacher of arithmetic. I do not keep accounts.

Jagmal: Children, too.

Bade Sarkar: Women and children, too.

Jagmal: Five pregnant women.

Bade Sarkar: I killed them with my own hands. Those children they would give birth to would grow up to be Naxalites. Our enemies.

Jagmal: Looking at those dead women and children brought back memories of my dead mother.

Bade Sarkar: Why?

Jagmal: Shivdayo Singh, you do not know. When the zamindar killed her for one bigha of land, she was pregnant. Perhaps she would have given birth to my brother. Another warrior like me. But you...

Zamindar: (*Frightened*) Go. Get away. You aren't right in the head today.

Jagmal stops rubbing his hands. He takes his spear off his shoulder. In the door, the wife, a gun in her hands.

Jagmal: Only this day is my head clear. Seeing those five women with their stomachs ripped open, Shivdayo Singh, brought back my mother.

He raises his spear.

Wife: Stop. Stop there. Or I'll shoot.

Jagmal: *Jai Mahakaal.*

He leaps at the zamindar who ducks behind the sofa. The wife raises the gun to her shoulder. Freeze. The ghungroos and nagaada set up a terrifying rhythm.

Darkness.

Act Three

Scene 1

Apoorva's room. Sukant places two cups on the table. Both take sips.

Apoorva: Sukant dear, you make good tea.

Sukant: I cook well too. My mother taught me. She was never very well.

Apoorva: Never give anyone information that can be used against you.

Sukant: Against me?

Apoorva: You told me you cook. After marriage, won't I use that information against you? In the first days of love, we are all fools. We want to share everything, tell everything. The sun shines through all twenty-four hours, fuelled by our love. We should keep some things secret, some personal information a mystery.

Sukant: (*Sadly*) What days of love these are. Your face has gone pale.

Apoorva: There was no sunlight in the jail cell. Neither to bid me good morning nor to bid me good night.

Sukant: They didn't even let me meet you. Did anyone try...

Apoorva: No one tried to do anything, love. They were under orders. The sub-inspectors there are all sympathizers.

They would bring food from their homes on the quiet. They had all worked with SP Lakshman. They told me...

Sukant: What did they tell you?

Apoorva: Lakshman is the smartest and most dangerous of all the officers. He shows no anger, he does not raise his voice. He thinks, he thinks constantly, even when he sleeps. He has had special training in England with the SAS, to deal with the likes of us. He lives the life of the enemy, always staying two steps ahead. But I...

Sukant: You should leave and go away from here.

Apoorva: Where do I go, love? I have no one to go to. I might come running to you, though.

Sukant: To me? No, you would not come to me. I am hardly your dream man.

Apoorva: Who is a dream man, anyway? The fellow who will run to the chemist and get you some pills when you have a headache. When I saw you, you amazed me and then I became obsessed with you. And I knew you were my dream man, Sukant. When one falls in love, one goes to live in a walled city. You made my soul bloom. In my eyes, rain-wet trees began to leaf. I wanted to become an eagle, to fly to the ends of the sky. And then plummet to the earth like a dive bomber. I wanted to scoop you up and whisk you away to my nest. I turned into a lovelorn, lovesick girl. I turned from a body to a fragrance, a fragrance...

Sukant: When will....?

Apoorva: (*Sadly*) It will not happen. I know it will not happen. You cannot wish a dry river into spate. Life is a squeak with no echoes. Sometimes I would begin to dream when I would take your hand in mine. But dreams have a short life expectancy. When I think of our high and pure vow, the dreams return to darkness. And then we become Keats' knight. 'O, what can ail thee knight-at-arms, / alone and palely loitering? / The sedge has wither'd from the lake, / And no birds sing.'

Sukant: If I cause you so much pain, I'll go...

Apoorva: Don't talk nonsense. As long as I am here, you will be with me, by my side. Or I'll kill...

Sukant: I know. You people kill those who love. As you did that zamindar's son, what was his name...?

Apoorva: A grand name if ever there was one. Aniruddh Pratapsingh. Whenever we met, he always talked to me in English, the language of the elite. He did a good job of pretending to sympathize with my beliefs. From the beginning, I knew his goal was the conquest of my body. My refusals were only a challenge. And the ruling class can never resist a challenge. Then he tried to bribe me, with a house and fifty thousand a month, to be his mistress. Then he began to threaten me. In Hindi now. These people know how to use language as a weapon. Then he raped three women who worked in the fields. All this to warn me. But why would I fear a bandmaster dressed up as a warrior. He was killed in those very fields. When the axe split his head open, he screamed in much the same way that the women he had raped screamed.

Sukant: A legal case could have been filed against him...

Apoorva: What law are you talking about? If we had gone to the police station, the case would not have been registered. If the matter had at all reached the court, no witnesses would have turned up. If the witnesses did show up, the judges would have had their empty pockets filled. They are all part of the same system. This is the first rule of being a man—you fight your own battles. You do not look with pleading eyes at other people.

Sukant: Life itself seems dangerous.

Apoorva: Which is why we have become dangerous. Now listen. I may have to go away for a few days...

Sukant: No. Wherever you're going, I'll come with you. You were the one who said the SP...

Apoorva: Yes, we have to keep an eye on him. Now we do not even mention names or places amongst ourselves. I will have to go, Sukant. And it may take me a little while before...

Sukant: What job can it be that will take you away for an unspecified amount of time? Killing someone. Tell me who. I will...

Apoorva: Being romantic gets you nowhere in a war. Sentiment only weakens one. I have to go alone. You'll have to wait...

Sukant: What am I to do? Wait helplessly? Poor helpless Sukant.

Apoorva: No one is helpless. Is the first ray of the sun helpless despite its pale yellow face? It rips the heart out of the darkness. Is the babble of the baby futile? It binds her mother to her with loops of iron. Is the old man, bent with the age, tottering along with the help of a stick, helpless? Against the battering of the storm, he reaches home. Are the leaves spinning in the wind futile? Is the poem you remember at the last moment of life futile? Is Sukant useless if his love for Apoorva makes him ready to kill. No. No one is helpless except for Apoorva. When she teases him, Sukant gets angry. No one is helpless except for Apoorva who could give Sukant no happiness. One day that chatterbox of a girl will fall silent. That's when you will be helpless. I...

Enter Naren.

Naren: Suryaswami has come. Are you ready?

Enter Suryaswami. He hesitates when he sees Sukant.

Suryaswami: Who is this?

Naren: Dr Sukant. Our sympathizer.

Suryaswami: These people can betray...

Apoorva: Suryaswami, Sukant is my friend. I have complete faith in him.

Suryaswami: Right. It's your risk (*he proffers the bag*). Everything's here. Including the passport. Go where you can. Germany or Sri Lanka. We'll figure it out later.

Sukant: Passport. You're running away abroad? No. I won't let...

Apoorva: (*Taking the passport out of the bag*) Here. Keep it. Where's the time or the opportunity to run?

Surya: You will have to leave the city in a bullock cart.

Then a motorcycle. The SP's men are watching the railway station, the bus stand and the taxi stand. Be very careful. SP Lakshman is our most intelligent enemy. I will mislead him tonight. After the zamindar's death, he gathered all the Veer Sena in one village. He thinks there's safety in numbers. Fools. They'll just die together.

Sukant: They have automatic weapons...

Surya: Those will be taken from them. Comrades from Andhra have arrived with the latest weapons. (*To Apoorva*) Leave now.

Apoorva: Getting to Delhi...

Surya: No, he's coming here. With the human rights people. He will be in the government guest house. And now hear this. Pay careful attention. No one will use his name. No one will even use the name of the city in which he is going to give his lecture.

Apoorva: But where do I...?

Surya: You will be taken to that city by motorcycle. Now there will be no contact between us. No telephone calls. No messages. Our people will be close to the guest house. Go, Apoorva, go.

Apoorva stops in front of Sukant.

Apoorva: Do not get angry with me so often. The day I get angry...

She leaves quickly. We hear ghungroos playing a sad snatch of music.

Surya: Dr Sukant, you will stay at the hospital for three days and nights. You will not leave it for even a moment.

Sukant: Because you will attack the Veer Sena today.

Surya: Yes and no. But you need witnesses. The patients. The chowkidaar. Whoever.

Sukant: Suryaji.

Surya: Yes, doctor. Ask. Ask without fear.

Sukant: I could kill...

Surya: Do not use his name. You wishing him dead won't kill him. The decision is made by committee. Apoorva is the best. She must do this. (*To all of them*) Okay, we are moving out for the attack.

Sukant: When will I hear from Apoorva? When will she return?

Surya: One of us will let you know. (*Puts a hand on Sukant's shoulder*) She will never come back. Sorry. Really sorry.

Sad music.

Exit severally.

Light grows and dims by turn. We see Sukant in his dispensary. In one corner of the stage, we hear a conversation.

Daroga: Sir, these people have attacked the Veer Sena in the village...

SP Lakshman: Good. Let them kill each other. The police force will remain a kilometre away from the village. Do you understand?

Daroga: Thirty people died in a hand grenade attack. The others ran for it, abandoning their weapons. Those people are pursuing them through the jungle. They're finishing them off with their own automatic weapons...

Silence.

SP: Oh my God, Suryaswami must be leading this. The most dreaded guerrilla fighter in the country. Was Apoorva part of the attack?

Daroga: No idea, sir. Our people did not spot her.

SP: How would they? Apoorva won't be there. This attack is Suryaswami's idea of diversionary tactics. Apoorva is somewhere else. On another mission.

Daroga: But the Prime Minister is not here...

SP: These people do not waste time with prime ministers. It will be a class enemy. Only who? (*He begins to pace*) Apoorva, you cannot outfox me. Who do you write your tirades against? Who is the target of your ire?

He stops, his hand to his head. Silence for a few moments. He moves his hand away. Straightens up.

SP: I know. Apoorva, you are finally dead. (*To the Daroga*) Who is coming on behalf of the human rights people?

Daroga: It's that retired judge, what's his name...

SP: Don't use his name. Nor the city to which he is coming. They must have an informer in the police force. How far away is it?

Daroga: Two hundred kilometres, sir. And a very poor road. Should we call the police there...

SP: No. Apoorva will get wind of it. She'll vanish. I'll catch her myself.

Daroga: Sir, helicopter?

SP: The Chief Minister has taken it to Delhi. Ten men. No one is to know where we're going. They can be told when we make the arrest. Move in five minutes.

The two go. Nagaadas play. Light and darkness play on Sukant, as a way of showing the passage of time. Silence. Enter Naren running.

Sukant: Apoorva?

Naren: No idea. Run. Run away. Now there'll be mass arrests. We're going underground.

Sukant: Why should I run? I want to see Apoorva.

Naren: No. If Apoorva is caught, you will never be able to find her. They will keep her in an interrogation centre, perhaps in another state. First, they'll break her so that our movement will be broken. Whoever knows her will be arrested. Run. For God's sake run away, Doctor Sukant.

Naren races out. An inspector and policemen come in.

Inspector: You are under arrest, Dr Sukant.

Sukant pushes him over. He falls, hits his head on the floor, screams. The constable's first strike with his lathi hits Sukant's head. He sits down heavily on the floor. The nagaadas play a terrifying tune. The lathis fall constantly on Sukant's body. Now he is curled up on the floor. The nagaadas pick up tempo.

Darkness.

Scene 2

In a well-appointed room of a government rest house, a charming old man in good clothes reads the newspaper. At the door, a chowkidaar.

Chowkidaar: Judge Saahab, some woman wants to meet you.

Judge: Woman? Oh, you mean a lady. What does she want?

Chowkidaar: Sir, she says she is a judgement from the newspapers.

Judge: Not a judgement, a journalist. Send her in.

Enter Apoorva. She smiles. For a few moments, the judge looks at her. There is admiration in his eyes.

Apoorva: Sir, I'm Apoorva, a journalist.

Judge: Please sit down. Should I use Miss or Mrs?

Apoorva: Just Apoorva will do. I'm not married.

Judge: (*Smiles*) Why not? You are so beautiful. Are the men all stupid?

Apoorva: I'd make do with one. But that one, I fear, is a bit stupid.

Judge: Looking at a beautiful woman can turn ninety per cent of the men of this country into fools. And they will remain here, in this country. We can't send all the fools to Pakistan. The country would empty.

Apoorva: Sir, I'd like to interview you about the environment.

Judge: I know. Every foreign journalist who comes along wants to talk about that.

Apoorva: Sir, after your earth-shaking judgement...

Judge: I did nothing, Apoorva. I take no credit. When I read the public interest petition, I was much struck. I often thought God was guiding me. Everything that is beautiful, healthy seemed to be on the verge of being destroyed. When I was writing the judgement, it was perhaps around middle of the night. That night, it seemed as if my pen were guided by the hand of God.

Apoorva: Yes, sir, the world press did indeed cover it as if it were holy writ. After all, the press can scarcely ignore the word of God.

Judge: Let's be clear. Are you against the environment? Let's get our premises clear. Should I call you Apoorva or Apoorvaji?

Apoorva: How great you are, sir. The world's press clubs and Rotary clubs are all standing in line, asking you to address them and instead, here you are, in this backward and violent area. And then you agree to see me.

Judge: But you know I'm here on a human rights mission. After I retired, several social organizations...

Apoorva: Those sixty people who were killed...

Judge: We will get them compensation.

Apoorva: And the killers their punishment?

Judge: No. That is for the law. The justice system...

Apoorva: Those murderers will receive their punishment tonight.

Judge: What did you say? How will they be punished? They haven't even been arrested. The cases haven't started so...

Apoorva: The people's court will sentence them. When you have seen what has happened with your own eyes, what need of witnesses?

Judge: You are talking of political terrorism. Do not glorify it. It has ended in the Punjab; it will end in Kashmir. And it will end here. Let's forget about it. No digressions now. I'll have to give it to you, Apoorva. Your news resources are strong. Never mind. Are you against an improvement upon nature and cleanliness?

Apoorva: No, sir, but it should not become a fever with us. That's when we demolish the Babri Masjid. Think about it. That middle-aged widow had this fever. On the television and in the papers we talk about flora and fauna. We want to have nothing to do with God's greatest creation: the human being. When this fever gets hold of you, then you want to remain part of the media and the news. When your range of vision narrows, change, progress becomes a social disease.

Judge: So polluted air and filthy water are not harmful?

Apoorva: Of course they're harmful. But this environment thing has become a conspiracy of certain nations. Who generates more nuclear waste, ozone depleting gases and chemicals than America? We still remember the mass murders Union Carbide committed. Some childish things are said in the name of the environment. These images of green trees and lush grass, and through the lush grass, there wanders a tiger.

It becomes news when that tiger dies. It is never news when the goat dies. For its fate is to die for the tiger.

Judge: You should have been a judge, Apoorva. What arguments. What biting language! But if the mills and factories are shifted out of the cities to the villages, surely they will benefit from employment.

Apoorva: No, sir. This is a delusion. A fallacy. The successful worker will only come from the city. From the village, you will only get contract labourers. With the factory will come the liquor shop. The usurious bania and his establishment. And then they will be alienated from their land. Their daughters and wives will become ten-rupee whores. The police and the ruling class will brand them criminal tribes. Sir, the developed countries have made the environment into a bogeyman.

Judge: But we can look to them for guidance.

Apoorva: Not for guidance but for conspiracies. A conspiracy to stop progress. In 1972, there was a conference at the UNO. America could not tolerate the rate at which Brazil was developing. Brazil's growth threatened America's export market. Which was when Brazil growled and announced: Smoke is the symbol of progress.

Judge: Great, Apoorva, great. You have your facts right.

Apoorva: Perhaps you do not remember that your Prime Minister also belonged to that conference. Do you know what she said—Poverty is the biggest polluter.

Judge: So you're against...

Apoorva: No, sir. The environment is everyone's business. Who does not like the idea of lush forests? Who does not like the idea of pure water with fish swimming free? Or the wind rich with the scent of flowers? Leaves shining in the sun and birds fluttering by? Or the cheeks of children flaming with blazing embers? But what can I do, sir? Over all these, I would value the human being.

Judge: Yes. That is precisely what I wrote in my judgement. The central concern of environmental activism is the human being.

Apoorva: Wrong. Your concern is for the five per cent, the golden five per cent, the elites, the aristocratic class.

Judge: Now you are talking nonsense.

Apoorva: The ruling class always calls the truth nonsense. How many factories did your ruling close down in the capital? Eighty thousand people lost their jobs.

Judge: The public interest petition did not just have...

Apoorva: You got your friends to file this incomplete public interest petition. There was no demand to set up factories in other places.

Judge: (*Angrily*) Do you know what your accusation means? Why would I do this?

Apoorva: Because three sets of people would benefit. The land owners who could sell the land at the prices they named. The builders who would construct five-star apartment towers in the heart of the capital. Your friends grew rich on this. Up to now five unemployed workers have killed themselves. Have you read that piece of news?

Judge: Non-persons keep on dying. Who reads news like that?

Apoorva: Yes, sir. It won't be long before ninety per cent of the people are declared non-persons. They will be like two-legged animals, for whom there will be no room in the country. Five other similar petitions have been filed. It's a conspiracy to turn more and more human beings into non-persons.

Judge: The court must decide on merit.

Apoorva: It should. Only it decides on bribes.

Judge: What bribes are you talking about? Do you know the punishment for a false accusation levelled at a judge?

Apoorva: Not a judge, sir. A retired judge. A non-person.

Judge: (*Sadly*) You're right. Only...

Apoorva: What happened to those thirty crores?

Judge: What thirty crores? (*Angrily*)

Apoorva: The thirty crores you went to Singapore to receive. Which were then stashed away in a foreign bank.

Judge: Don't talk nonsense. Who says...?

Apoorva: Everyone knows. But no one is going to catch you. After all, they will themselves be exposed.

Judge: What can be done now? You are very late.

Apoorva: Things can be done. Petitions can be dismissed...

Judge: Rubbish. You cannot terrorize a judge.

Apoorva: (*Opening her purse*) Can't I? I can by killing you. Killing someone who has sentenced eighty thousand workers to slow death.

The nagaada begins to play, a frightening sound.

Judge: Don't kill me. Please don't kill me. I will tender a public apology. You won't escape. Where will you...?

Apoorva: I won't run.

Judge: Then you'll be...

Apoorva: Which is why I won't run. You do not announce a war and then run and hide. Now we will be face to face. So that your enemies will be afraid. Now you yourself are a non-person. The country has no need of you. And so I sentence you to death on eighty thousand counts for having sent these workers and their families to a living death.

Outside, swift running footsteps. Apoorva puts the revolver to the judge's temple. Enter SP and Daroga.

SP: No, Apoorva, no, don't shoot.

Apoorva: (*Smiles*) Sir, you've arrived a little too late.

Freeze. Nagaada plays a victorious beat.

Darkness.

Scene 3

Meeting room in a jail. An ordinary table with chairs on either side. A bench against the wall. No decorations at all. Suryaswami, Naren and three boys, standing silently. Sukant sits on a bench; a huge bruise on his head. The sound of footsteps. Two warders arrive and stand at the door. Apoorva enters. She is in a prison-inmate sari, her hair tied back. The gentle tinkle of ghungroos. It rises and then stops abruptly. Everyone goes to her quickly. They take her hand one by one.

Suryaswami: How are you, Apoorva?

Apoorva: (*Smiles*) You see me, a resplendent beggar. Inside, summer sings.

Apoorva sees Sukant. She goes quickly to him, sees the bruises.

Apoorva: Who did this? Who dared to hit you?

No one answers. A short silence.

Apoorva: Why won't you speak? Who did this to him? And where were you?

Youth 1: The police did it.

Youth 2: They came to arrest him. The sub-inspector got his head broken. And that's when the lathis fell.

Apoorva turns to Sukant.

Apoorva: The case has dragged on for months. And you haven't come to see me once. You were scared.

Naren: Doctor Saahab was in jail. He got six months for attacking a policeman.

Apoorva: Why wasn't I told?

Surya: You know very well that we do not give out such news.

Apoorva: In jail, Sukant...

Surya: He took a lot of beating. But then Doctor Saahab has turned violent. Some warder abused him once. He beat him up. Now he beats the doctor every day. And the doctor here takes every chance to get back to him. He can barely walk now. His leg...

Apoorva shakes Sukant.

Apoorva: Get up. Walk and show me. (*Sukant gets up and walks.*) They broke his leg. You people should have killed...

Naren: We warned him. We went to his house and threatened him. We had to tell him we would kill his children. That was when they stopped the beating.

Apoorva: (*Puts a hand on Sukant's shoulder*) What have I done? I did not tell you to become so dangerous.

The ghungroos sound sadly. Sukant returns to the bench.

Apoorva: Why aren't you talking to me, love? I haven't the time to coax you out of your anger. Please don't turn away from me, Sukant. Please don't be angry.

Naren: He's angry that he was not given the opportunity to kill that judge. He says we do not trust him. That you betrayed him.

Apoorva: I did not betray you, love. I did not fall in love with anyone in jail. Oh yes, the jailer does seem to love me. He's lost his voice asking me to appeal.

Youth 3: The doctor says he too could...

Apoorva: Sukant, it's not enough to want to kill someone. You can't change a fuse; how would you have used a gun? Have you ever seen one? Touched one? Do you know what would have happened if you had been sent? I'll tell you. You would have been caught and he would have escaped. Taking a life is not easy. First you have to fight a long battle within yourself. It is difficult to kill.

Warder: The jailer is coming.

Enter the jailer wearing good clothes. He goes to Apoorva.

Jailer: Outside on the maidan, thousands of people have gathered. Adivasis, workers, men, women and children. All silent. They are not talking to each other either. Surely they're not going to try and save Apoorva by launching an attack...

Surya: They will not attack. It has been explained to them. The city will be under curfew tonight. Two battalions of the Rapid Action Force will come in. No one will be allowed to get out. And so they have come out of their houses before the curfew tolls. To take Apoorva's dead body away. To perform the last rites.

Jailer: Apoorva, you have not told us to whom your dead body is to be given. I have to inform the Home Secretary.

Apoorva: (*Smiles*) What wishes can a dead person have? You may burn it yourself. They will pay for the wood.

Jailer: (*In an almost-shout*) You will hang tomorrow and you're smiling. One does not laugh at death, Apoorva. You are a cruel woman. I ask you: do you not fear death?

Apoorva touches the jailer's hand.

Apoorva: I fear death, sir. I fear it terribly. I am not an unfeeling woman.

Jailer: Then why don't you appeal...?

Apoorva: No. We do not appeal. It is always the poor and the unarmed who are given death sentences. If you don't believe me, look at the records of the last ten years. Has a rich man ever been hanged? The rich hire the best lawyers, the best lawyers find a loophole or a new interpretation and the death sentence gets transmuted to a few years of jail. And the jail cell in the capital slowly acquires a television, a computer, a phone and food comes in from good hotels and those few years pass quite merrily. It is part of the same system against which we are fighting.

Warder: (*To the jailer*) Sir, SP Saahab is coming.

The jailer and the warder straighten up. SP Lakshman walks in, his gait crisp. He goes to Apoorva and touches her head.

SP: I am sorry. I am really sorry, Apoorva. May God be with you.

Apoorva: (*Sadly*) He has already left me, sir. (*To Suryaswami*) Take my Sukant to some other state where he can practise. (*And in the tone of an order*) Hear this. You must not let Sukant die.

Surya: Death does not take geography into account. We all have an appointment in Samarra.

Apoorva goes to Sukant.

Apoorva: You haven't combed your hair.

Sukant is silent.

Apoorva: Listen, Sukant, I do not believe in family planning.

Everyone looks at her, surprised.

Apoorva: If I had married you, I would have given you seven sons and a daughter.

Youth 1: Such a big family.

Apoorva: Yes. The seven brothers would protect him. Who could give him the death sentence then?

The ghungroos sound, sadly.

Apoorva: Say something, Sukant. Say something. When the noose is put around my neck, I will remember the last word of the last sentence you speak. (*And then in a terrified voice*) Stop me, Sukant. Please stop me.

Sukant rises, limps up to her, puts his hand on her shoulder.

Sukant: Now who can stop you? Who has the power to stop you? You must go forward. For you have become the saddest poem ever written. A woman is the saddest poem. The worker who struggles forever and fails forever is the saddest poem. The woman who gives birth in the fields is the saddest poem. Poverty is the saddest of all poems. When a chatty girl suddenly falls silent, it is the saddest poem. The last words of a dying man become the saddest poem.

A short silence. Sad music. Apoorva looks at Sukant and then at the others. She begins to recite the poem with increasing confidence:

Come and enfold me in your shawl, spun of the yarn of
  darkness.
Come, sleep that will close my lids forever, come.
Come, salesman of my last breaths.
Come, evil hag, intent on wiping the slate
of my eyes clean of every last scene, come.
Come, for you have nothing left to take.
Come, for you may take nothing but this body.
Come, for this body has completed every vow required of it.
Come, for every file is filled.

Come, for every letter has been answered.
Come, for injustice has been protested,
And revenge taken.
Come, for I may have no love of you.
But come, for now I have no fear of you.

A complete silence. Apoorva, now sitting at the table, puts her head on it. All heads bow. Sukant stares fixedly in front of him. Suryaswami goes to Apoorva. He puts his hand on her head. Apoorva looks at him.

Surya: The sun sets but it always rises again. A child is born, grows and fights. We are in the habit of fighting long wars. And the battle never stops just because someone dies. Remember that. As Shakespeare says: Cowards die a thousand deaths, the brave die only once.

Apoorva rises. Her face is full of pride and victory. She unties her hair, shakes it out. It falls over her shoulders. The light dims. A spotlight on Apoorva. She begins to speak.

One person's death does not stop anything
One person's death does not stop the struggle
When a leaf falls, a new seedling sprouts
The sky fills with a flight of new birds
New fish are born in the rivers
Green spreads far and wide
In the dust, the footsteps of a new generation
Death stops nothing
Death halts nothing
Life goes on, endlessly

The light begins to dim. Apoorva's face has a familiar smile. Darkness.

Curtain.

Court Martial

Translated by Pratik Kanjilal and Nirupama Dutt

Cast

Colonel Surat Singh: Presiding judge
Major Ajay Puri: Prosecution lawyer
Captain Bikash Roy: Defence counsel
Judge Advocate: Unnamed
Other Judges: Unnamed
Ramchandra: Accused
Subedar Balwan Singh, Dr Captain Gupta, Captain B.D. Kapoor, Lt Col Brajendra Rawat: Witnesses
Guard/Sentry: Unnamed

~

Time: The Present
Place: Court Martial Room
Act One: First Day
Act Two: Second Day

Act One

The entry is from the left wing of the stage, through a small passage. A plywood frame with four windows lines the passage. The characters entering or exiting the stage will be visible through these windows. The frame conveys the illusion of a wall. At times, the windows will frame the faces of the characters as they converse among themselves. The characters in the window frames will not serve as a chorus but rather as the voice of dissent and criticism. Past the windows, which are initially closed, is an arched doorway guarded by a sentry.

The Action Begins: The darkened stage resounds with the tread of heavy army boots. The sentry is pacing up and down the passage, but is not visible in the darkness. He looks brisk in his uniform and is armed with a Sten gun. He continues marching and we hear the sound of his boots. There is a slightly raised platform at stage right with a long table and chairs for the judges. Below, on either side of the platform are two chairs, one for the prosecution lawyer and the other for the defence counsel. Facing the platform are a few chairs for the witnesses, and for soldiers and officers.

At centre stage is a big revolving chair. A person enters the stage in the darkness and takes the chair. He fills his pipe with tobacco. There is the rasp of a lighter. In the momentary glow, the audience gets only a glimpse of his face. He takes a long drag and gradually exhales. Slowly, the lights come up.

The man gets up from his chair and, one by one, opens the four closed windows.

He stands by the witness box, an enclosure made with four bamboo poles and some rope. The man takes another long pull on his pipe. As he exhales the smoke, the stage lights dim and a spot focuses on him. Under the spotlight, he starts speaking, as if addressing the audience.

Colonel Surat Singh: I am Col Surat Singh, presiding officer of this court martial. Have you ever confronted death? Perhaps not. I have faced death many times, in the battlefield and in court martial rooms. The moments when death stares you in the face have the power to freeze your blood—or to set it aflame. I am not talking from the perspective of an invalid in a sickbed. I am talking of Death poised for the fateful leap. Death that can be seen so clearly, even if it is only for a moment. In the eyes of the killer and in the eyes of the victim.

I have killed many people, snuffed out their lives. In battle and in courts martial. But not once did my blood freeze or burn with rage. Perhaps in those moments my ancestors came to dwell in my soul. They have played the game of death for centuries. They are dealers in death.

The characters in my grandmother's tales have become a part of my being: eager riders wielding naked swords, galloping day and night across fields, deserts and mountains—the riders of death. Horses thundering across the hot sands, the sound of swords slashing flesh, the blood seeping into the sand. Before Independence, we ruled a small principality in Rajasthan.

My grandmother would tell me these tales of my grandfather. The stories of a bandit king. I am not talking of my father, who never mounted a horse and went out to kill. He was happy just hitting the ball about at the polo ground. I am not talking of my mother either, because she belongs to this age too—a Coca-Cola product.

Grandmother would tell me that our ancestors wielded swords in both hands. They never accepted or understood the concept of holding a sword in one hand and a cup of water in the other. They knew neither compassion nor forgiveness. Me? I never forgive, nor do I show compassion of any kind.

He draws at his pipe, but it has gone cold. He lights up again, but then pauses in thought and extinguishes the pipe. He sucks on the unlit pipe and continues:

Memories of the last war are still fresh in my mind. Such terrifying memories. With just three soldiers left alive, we attacked the enemy's post. The Gurkha soldiers of my unit with their khukris, slashing the heads of the enemies. And I, Captain Surat Singh, plucking grenades from my bandoliers and lobbing them one after the other. Yes, I was a captain then. A foreign journalist had published my picture with the caption, 'The Lion with Grenades'. In the army, they called me 'Grenade Singh'—not to my face, of course. Seeing death in the eyes of the enemy was a truly joyous moment. Have you ever enjoyed the bliss of such moments? Perhaps not.

For us, such moments come in the battlefield or during a court martial. But no one has ever been able to lay a trap for

Surat Singh. Neither in battle nor in a court martial. I know the art of escaping traps. I move as silently as a cheetah and then, with a mighty roar, I leap like a tiger upon my prey. A murderous leap. Only once have I failed. Only once.

I was totally disarmed. It was not wartime; no enemy faced me. Both swords fell from my hands. For the first time, my grandmother's tales seemed like lies. Absolute lies. For the first time I learned the horrifying truth—that when we kill, a part of us dies too. Is truth only that which we can comprehend? Is truth only what meets the eye? Certainly not. Truth is an ember in the palm of your hand, a glowing ember. Have you ever tried to hold this ember? Perhaps not. I, Col Surat Singh, held this live coal in my hand. Just once...

He goes to the revolving chair and lights his pipe. Then, with a sudden jerk, he sets the chair spinning. He stares at the revolving chair for a while, then slowly walks offstage. Two soldiers enter in dim light.

First Soldier: (*Putting files on the table*) Nothing on earth can save Ramchandra now. When Col Surat Singh is the presiding officer of a court martial, no one can get away. Just impossible!

Second Soldier: (*Putting a chair in front of the platform erected on the stage*) Is Colonel Saahab a very strict officer?

First Soldier: You're a new recruit, or you wouldn't ask. He has presided over as many as ten courts martial. Ten, I tell you, and not a single accused has escaped him. We may as well say the last prayers for Ramchandra.

Uniformed officers and soldiers enter. The four judges take their seats, leaving the chair in the middle vacant. A guard leads a soldier to the chair in front of the platform, and then returns to his post at the arched doorway. Two officers seat themselves in the chairs on either side of the platform. One is the prosecution lawyer and the other is the defence counsel. The stage is now fully lit. Through the four open windows, we see someone coming. The guard stiffens and clicks his heels loudly.

Guard: (*Shouldering his rifle, shouts*) Attention!

The guard salutes Col Surat Singh. All the officers and soldiers in the courtroom rise. They click their heels and salute the colonel. The colonel returns the salute. Everyone stands at attention. Col Surat Singh slowly surveys the room. He looks stern, his face stony. He walks to the platform. One officer judge pulls back the vacant chair and the Colonel sits down. Everyone is still standing. The Colonel throws them another stern glance. He picks up the file in front of him. The four judges also pick up their files.

Surat Singh: Sit down. (*To one of the officers who are seated below the platform*) Maj Ajay Puri, start the court martial proceedings.

Major Ajay Puri, prosecution lawyer, rises and walks up to the chair at centre stage. The soldier sitting in the chair bows his head. A spotlight falls on him. The soldier is lean but strongly built. His face is pale in the bright light. The spotlight will remain on the soldier as long as Maj Puri speaks.

Major Ajay Puri: (*Pointing to the soldier in the chair*)

On the night of June 10, Jawan Ramchandra was on sentry duty. At 9 pm, two officers of the regiment, Capt Mohan Verma and Capt Kapoor, went past the sentry post on a motorcycle. Jawan Ramchandra shot at them with his service rifle. Capt Verma died on the spot and Capt Kapoor was grievously injured. Capt Kapoor survived because the bullet hit him near the left shoulder. But if he had not been rushed to the military hospital and operated upon, he could have died too. The medical report states that if the bullet had hit him two inches lower, in the region of the heart, there would have been no question of his survival. This shows that Jawan Ramchandra had premeditated the killing of these two officers. The accused is being prosecuted under Indian Army Act 69 and the Indian Penal Code, Section 302. He is facing a general court martial for cold-blooded murder committed while he was in complete control of himself.

Maj Puri returns to his chair. The spotlight leaves the soldier and shifts to the others on the stage. Everyone is stony-faced. Col Surat Singh bends towards a judge sitting by his side and asks him something. The judge nods in affirmation.

Surat Singh: (*Looking at the accused*) This general court martial is being held for the cold-blooded and premeditated murder of Capt Verma and the murderous attack on Capt Kapoor. Do you confess to your crime? How do you plead? Guilty or not guilty!

Ramchandra: (*Gets up and clicks his heels*) Sir! Sir!

Surat Singh: Sit down, Jawan Ramchandra. (*Turning to the prosecutor*) Maj Puri, present the first witness.

Before Maj Puri can begin, the defence counsel rises from his chair and approaches Col Surat Singh.

Surat Singh: Yes, Capt Bikash Roy, what is the problem?

Captain Bikash Roy: Before Maj Puri presents the first witness, I must say something.

Surat Singh: (*Sarcastically*) The court martial has not begun yet, but Capt Roy's objections have. Speak on.

Bikash Roy: Maj Puri addressed the accused twice as Jawan Ramchandra.

Surat Singh: (*Cutting him short*) So what? What should he say?

Bikash Roy: Major Puri should have addressed him as Sawar Ramchandra.

Surat Singh: What's this? What the hell do you mean? Isn't Ramchandra a jawan of the army? What difference does it make if he is called Jawan Ramchandra or Sawar Ramchandra?

Bikash Roy: There is a difference, sir! You are a colonel of the infantry. Now, I cannot call you a colonel of the medical service. Ramchandra is from an armoured regiment and tradition demands that he should be called Sawar, not Jawan.

Judge Advocate: (*Nodding to Surat Singh*) Capt Roy is right. The prosecutor should have called him Sawar Ramchandra. (*He turns to Bikash Roy with an ironic smile*) Perhaps the defence counsel will want the court martial order annulled on technical grounds.

Bikash Roy: Can there be a technical loophole when the Law Department of the Army has deputed a senior officer like you as Judge Advocate? Matters of life and death are not decided on technical grounds, but by the truth. And truth always speaks for itself. A lie is always found out.

Surat Singh: Capt Roy, restrict yourself to what is relevant to the court martial proceedings against Jawan Ramchandra... I mean Sawar Ramchandra. (*Glances harshly at everyone in the court*) Capt Roy and everyone else should remember that this is a court martial, not a Hindi film. The time of the court should not be wasted with irrelevant details. Is that clear to all? The presiding officer of this court martial is Surat Singh, Col Surat Singh. Don't you ever forget that!

Bikash Roy: Sir! The Judge Advocate has also sustained my objection that the accused be called Sawar Ramchandra. I am sorry if you feel that a rightful objection amounts to waste of the court's time. If you feel that I am objecting to irrelevant matters, you can appoint another officer to appear as defence counsel. I shall return to Delhi.

Absolute silence in the courtroom. Surat Singh stares at Bikash Roy.

Surat Singh: Don't you threaten me. Everyone knows that Ramchandra is the murderer. Even the newspapers have reported it. Ramchandra has actually confessed to his crime. I know, you know, and everyone in this court knows who the murderer is. Isn't Ramchandra on trial here, whether you call him Jawan Ramchandra or Sawar Ramchandra?

Bikash Roy: Sir, you have decided who the murderer is even before the trial has begun! Then why have a court martial? What is the need for this farce? If you wish, I shall submit, in writing, my refusal to plead this case since the court has already decided the matter. Besides, it is not necessary, not at all necessary, that all newspaper reports are true. The printed word has a habit of prevaricating.

Judge Advocate: Sit down, Capt Roy. (*Glancing at Maj Puri*) You may present the first witness.

Maj Puri: (*Reads from the file*) The first witness in this case is Subedar Balwan Singh.

A middle-aged, strongly-built man gets up and walks briskly to the witness box. His chest is decorated with several medals.

Maj Puri: Subedar Saahab, where were you at 9 pm on the night of June 10?

Balwan Singh: Sir, I was near the regiment's guardhouse.

Maj Puri: What were you doing there at night? Were you on night duty?

Balwan Singh: No, sir, I was not on duty. My quarters are near the guardhouse. There was a power cut that night. It was very warm. So I was taking a walk with Havildar Raj Singh in the field near the guardhouse.

Maj Puri: Who was on guard duty that night?

Balwan Singh: Jawan...I mean, Sawar Ramchandra.

Maj Puri: What did you see at 9 pm on the night of June 10?

Balwan Singh: Sir, I just told you that the lights were

out, so I could not see anything clearly. A motorcycle came past the sentry post...

Maj Puri: (*Interrupting him*) You couldn't see clearly! Perhaps you were not wearing your glasses.

Balwan Singh: (*Thrusting his chest out*) Sir! My vision is absolutely all right. I do not wear glasses.

Maj Puri: But you just said that you could not see very clearly...

Balwan Singh: Sir, there was a power cut.

Maj Puri: Subedar Saahab, what if the lights were out? June 10 was the night of the full moon. You were strolling about a hundred metres from the guardhouse. In the light of the full moon, there is clear visibility for up to four or five hundred metres. You should have been able to see even a small ball lying in the field. But never mind. How many riders did you see on the motorcycle that went past the sentry post?

Balwan Singh: Two.

Maj Puri: Were they wearing helmets?

Balwan Singh: No.

Maj Puri: Then you must have recognized them both?

Balwan Singh: Yes, sir! Capt Verma was driving and Capt Kapoor was riding pillion.

Maj Puri: All right. If you could recognize the two officers of your regiment from such a distance, then Ramchandra, who was on guard duty, must have recognized them too.

Balwan Singh: Yes, sir!

Maj Puri: What did you see then?

Balwan Singh: When the motorcycle neared the sentry post, Ramchandra opened fire. The first bullet hit Capt Verma. The motorcycle careened off the road and hit a tree a little ahead of the sentry post. As the motorcycle reeled, Ramchandra fired again.

Balwan Singh pauses for breath. The spotlight is on an officer sitting in a chair, stiffly arrogant. The nameplate on his chest says: 'B.D. Kapoor'.

Maj Puri: Then? What happened then?

Balwan Singh: The second bullet hit Capt Kapoor below his shoulder. The motorcycle fell down. Ramchandra ran towards it and raised his gun again to fire. By then Havildar Raj Singh and I had run to the spot. We grabbed Ramchandra from behind.

Maj Puri: When you grabbed Ramchandra, who was he aiming at?

Balwan Singh: At the injured Capt Kapoor.

Maj Puri: Which means that if you had not rushed and grabbed Ramchandra, he would have murdered the wounded Capt Kapoor too?

Balwan Singh: Yes, sir!

Maj Puri: What happened after that?

Balwan Singh: On hearing the shots, several jawans came racing out of their barracks. They reached the spot too. Ramchandra was screaming, 'I fired the shots. Leave me alone, let me go, I say. I'll kill this captain too!' But by that time, we had snatched the rifle from his hands. With great difficulty, four or five of us managed to overpower him. God knows, saahab, from where Ramchandra drew that terrible strength that night.

The spotlight falls on Ramchandra. He sits with his head bowed, his chin almost touching his chest. He knows that everyone in the courtroom is staring at him. Maj Puri is lost in thought for some time. Then he turns towards the witness box.

Maj Puri: (*Standing in front of Col Surat Singh*) I do not wish to question the witness further.

He returns to his seat and looks at Capt Bikash Roy, his eyes victorious.

Advocate Judge: Capt Roy, you may question the witness.

Bikash Roy rises. He walks slowly to Capt Kapoor's chair and stops. Capt Kapoor looks at him in surprise. They stare at each other. Capt Kapoor lowers his gaze. Bikash Roy circles Capt Kapoor's chair. The spotlight is now on the guard standing by the arched doorway, who stands alert. Then it moves back to Capt Kapoor. The guard is staring at Capt Kapoor. Bikash Roy strides forward and stands before Subedar Balwan Singh. The guard, now at ease, is still staring at Capt Kapoor.

Bikash Roy: Subedar Saahab! Since when have you known Ramchandra?

Balwan Singh: Sir, I've know him for three years, ever since Ramchandra was posted to our regiment from the Training Centre.

Bikash Roy: In these three years, has Ramchandra ever got into a brawl with anyone? Has there ever been a complaint against him?

Balwan Singh: Not at all, sir! Not even an argument with anyone. He is a good man.

Bikash Roy: Did Ramchandra ever shirk any duty that you or another officer may have assigned him?

Balwan Singh: Never, sir. Ramchandra always performed his duties efficiently. There has never been a complaint against him.

Bikash Roy: Did Capt Mohan Verma, who is no more, or Capt Kapoor, ever complain against him? Did they take any action against him? Or did they punish him in any way?

Balwan Singh: No, sir!

Bikash Roy turns and looks at Col Surat Singh and the other judges. Then he turns back to look at all the others in the room. The guard standing in the arch moves from his place. The sound of his heavy boots breaks the silence. Bikash Roy walks up to Capt Kapoor's chair. He asks the next question from this position.

Bikash Roy: (*Stressing every word*) Then why did he kill Capt Mohan Verma? Why did he try to kill Capt Kapoor?

Balwan Singh: (*Surprised*) How would I know this, sir? I am just relating what I saw.

Bikash Roy: Subedar Saahab, is the truth only as much as one can see? We see only a part of the truth with our eyes, and tend to believe it is the whole truth. Then, it is also not necessary that what you or I see is the truth.

Balwan Singh: No, sir! What the eye sees is always the truth.

Bikash Roy: (*Smiles*) Really! Is the spot where you are standing moving? Is it turning?

Balwan Singh: No.

Bikash Roy: Is this courtroom moving? Is it turning?

Balwan Singh: No.

Bikash Roy: You are saying only what you see, aren't you? And what your eyes can see is not true. Absolutely untrue. You know that the earth is spinning all the time. It rotates on its own axis and revolves around the sun. Just because you cannot see it happen does not mean that it is not true.

Subedar Balwan Singh is silent. Everyone looks at Bikash Roy in amazement. The guard's eyes are on him.

Maj Puri: What is the connection between the earth's rotation and this case? Capt Roy is deliberately trying to confuse the witness. He has the right to ask only those questions which concern this trial.

Surat Singh: Maj Puri is right, Capt Roy. Do your questions have any bearing on the trial? I have already warned that no one has the right to waste the time of the court.

Bikash Roy: Right, sir! Time is truly valuable. (*Looks at Ramchandra*) Even more valuable than a life. The court's concern is valid. Time should certainly not be wasted even if it means sending someone to the gallows in error. (*In a sober and soft voice*) Time and truth always move in opposite directions. Only the future can determine the truth. Truth is always a child of the future. (*Turning to the Judge Advocate*) I was just trying to explain that truth is neither so small nor so simple that it can be understood in a mere glance.

Surat Singh is staring fixedly at Bikash Roy. He picks up his pipe but instead of puffing at it, he begins to twist it with his other hand. The guard standing in the archway looks at Col Surat Singh first and then at Bikash Roy, before shifting his feet. The sound of his boots is heard.

Judge Advocate: Capt Roy! Would you like to ask the witness anything more?

Bikash Roy: (*Leaning towards the Subedar*) What was the secret password the night of the incident?

Balwan Singh: (*Surprised*) What? What are you asking?

Bikash Roy: (*Smiles*) I mean the password.

Judge Advocate: I suggest Capt Roy should use simple language so that he does not have to explain himself again.

A titter runs through the courtroom. Surat Singh looks around sternly and the laughter subsides.

Bikash Roy: Yes, saahab! What was the password that night?

Balwan Singh: I can't recall it, sir! If you permit me, I shall check it with the regiment clerk.

Bikash Roy: (*Consoling him*) Never mind, saahab! There is a new password every night. It may be difficult to recall the password for a particular night so many months ago. I shall tell you what it was. The password on that full moon night was Black Moon. You can confirm it with the regiment clerk.

Subedar bows his head, somewhat embarrassed. A soldier walks to Col Surat Singh with a register and opens it to a page. The Colonel shows the register to the other judges, closes it and puts it on the table. The soldier returns to his place.

Surat Singh: Correct. The password for that night was Black Moon. Subedar Saahab, you should have remembered it. You must remember everything concerning the night of the murder. (*Turning to Bikash Roy*) Continue, Captain!

Bikash Roy: Subedar Saahab, it has been established that you recognized the two officers riding a motorcycle at quite a distance. This means Ramchandra too must have recognized them and known that both were officers of his regiment.

Balwan Singh: Yes, sir! This is exactly what I am saying.

Bikash Roy: (*Smiling*) That is the truth. And all of us here have sworn to speak only the truth. Have you instructed the jawans that on recognizing an officer, they should not ask for the password?

Balwan Singh: (*A little annoyed*) Sir, who am I to give such an instruction? A rule is a rule. A guard is supposed to stop everyone and demand the password. I have a spotless service record of twenty years. (*Somewhat angrily*) Wouldn't I know something so simple?

Bikash Roy: I know that you know it. I know you would never give such an instruction. When the two officers on the motorcycle reached the sentry post, did Ramchandra challenge them? Did he shout: 'Halt, who goes there?'

Balwan Singh: No, sir! I saw it with my own eyes. If Ramchandra had shouted...

Bikash Roy: I am not talking of seeing, but hearing. Did you hear Ramchandra say, 'Halt, who goes there?'

Balwan Singh: I did not hear it. How can I confirm that he challenged them?

Bikash Roy walks to Capt Kapoor's chair, goes around it once and then stands facing Capt Kapoor. He asks his next question from there.

Bikash Roy: Do you mean to say that what you have not heard was not uttered at all? Tell me, were you in Delhi this August 15?

Balwan Singh: (*Surprised*) No. Why do you ask?

Bikash Roy: From the ramparts of the Red Fort, the Prime Minister declared that the enemies of India would be crushed. You were not in Delhi that day. You did not hear it with your own ears. However, this does not mean that the Prime Minister did not say this in his speech, just because you didn't hear it yourself.

Balwan Singh: Sir, I could see everything clearly...

Bikash Roy: (*In a raised voice*) A voice is *heard*, not seen. You were taking a walk some five hundred metres from the spot. From that distance, given the noise of a Bullet motorcycle, you could not have heard Sawar Ramchandra shout: 'Halt, who goes there?'

Balwan Singh: I was taking a walk a hundred metres away...

Bikash Roy: Maj Puri said that and you believed him. Did you measure the distance? I did. You were five hundred metres from the spot, not a hundred metres. You simply could not have heard Ramchandra shout.

The Subedar is lost in thought. He is silent. The guard's body stiffens into a posture of attack. The prosecutor, Maj Ajay Puri, rises from his chair.

Maj Puri: Capt Roy is deliberately confusing the witness. A question should be asked only once. He has agreed to the fact that Ramchandra had recognized the officers on the motorcycle. Why must he go on about whether he challenged them or not? What is the meaning of it all?

Bikash Roy: There is a meaning to it, Maj Puri! Who are you to question me? That is the right of the Presiding Officer, not yours.

Col Surat Singh consults the Judge Advocate, who nods in agreement.

Surat Singh: Capt Roy, continue with your questioning.

Bikash Roy walks away from Capt Kapoor's chair to the witness.

Bikash Roy: All right, Subedar Saahab, explain this to me. If someone does not stop when he is challenged, then...

Maj Puri: Capt Roy is deliberately twisting his questions. Why ask about something that never happened? When has it been established that Sawar Ramchandra had challenged the two officers or asked for the password? How can the witness tell him...?

Bikash Roy: That is exactly what I'm saying. How can the witness tell what he has not heard? He simply cannot. I request the court that we visit the spot at 9 pm tonight. The judges should stand where Subedar Saahab was taking a stroll. A motorcycle should be started and a soldier should shout the challenge from the sentry post. We shall learn if a challenge can be heard at that distance.

Surat Singh: Even if we did that, what would it prove? That Sawar Ramchandra had not fired those shots? That the murderous assault in which one officer was killed and another injured never took place?

Bikash Roy: Sir, who am I to prove that Ramchandra had not fired those shots? He has already confessed to having done so, in public. (*He walks to Capt Kapoor's chair*) But I wish to remind the court of the army rule that if someone does not stop on being challenged by the guard, the guard has the right to open fire.

Stunned silence. Surat Singh clenches his fists and roars at Bikash Roy.

Surat Singh: Don't try to teach this court the army law! You would teach law? You would teach *me*?

All present in the courtroom sit frozen in their seats. Bikash Roy goes up to Surat Singh. They look at each other. The Colonel is angry but Bikash Roy smiles. The Judge Advocate scribbles something and passes it to the Colonel. The Colonel reads it and tears the paper to bits. The tension and anger recede from the Colonel's face as he seems to reach a decision.

Surat Singh: (*Addressing the Judge Advocate*) Nothing will be done in stealth in this court. No chance. I want you to announce to everyone what you just advised me.

Judge Advocate: If it is proved that the officers did not stop after being challenged by Ramchandra, then, according to army law, he had the right to fire. It was his duty to shoot to kill.

Maj Puri: Everyone knows this law, but it is followed strictly only in wartime...

Surat Singh: (*Interrupting Maj Puri harshly*) Don't talk rubbish. There can't be separate laws for wartime and peacetime. Law is law, war or no war.

Judge Advocate: We should not go to the crime scene. The defence counsel is deliberately derailing the proceedings. When Ramchandra has already confessed that he committed the murder, knowing what he was doing, there is no point in giving so much importance to whether he challenged them or not.

Surat Singh: But why should we not go to the spot? This court martial aims to learn the truth, not conceal it. The court *will* go to the spot. It certainly will.

Judge Advocate: Then Ramchandra will be acquitted. He will certainly be acquitted, if it is established that the officers did not stop after being challenged or that they did not give the password or show their identity cards.

Surat Singh: (*Harshly*) Mister Judge Advocate! When did the court decide that Ramchandra must be sentenced to death, come what may?

Judge Advocate: But, sir...

Surat Singh: No ifs and buts. Who is the presiding officer of this court martial, you or I?

The Judge Advocate does not reply. Surat Singh looks around the room. Capt Kapoor, who has been sitting confidently so far, now shrinks in his seat. There is fear in his eyes. The Colonel looks at him and Capt Kapoor lowers his eyes. Capt Bikash Roy stands up. The Colonel looks at him in surprise, because there is no reason for him to stand up.

Surat Singh: Capt Roy, the court will visit the scene of the crime tonight at nine. We shall determine whether Ramchandra had challenged the officers.

Bikash Roy quickly goes to Ramchandra. They look at each other. Ramchandra's bowed head rises and there is a decisive gleam in his eyes. Bikash Roy nods. Ramchandra stands up.

Bikash Roy: I do not want the members of the court to go to the spot and waste their time. Ramchandra wants to say something...

Maj Puri: (*Getting up with a start*) No, Ramchandra cannot speak now. Subedar Saahab is already in the witness box...

Ramchandra: (*Speaks loudly and clearly*) Sir, I had not challenged them that night. I never said, 'Halt, who goes there!' I opened fire without challenging them.

Startled, all stand up, as if a bolt of electricity has passed through them. Col Surat Singh has almost risen too, but then sits down. Suddenly, Capt Kapoor starts speaking.

Capt Kapoor: The court may note this confession of Ramchandra. He opened fire without challenging.

Surat Singh: Sit down, Captain! Who the hell has made you the prosecutor?

Capt Kapoor sits down. Bikash Roy goes to Capt Kapoor, flashes him a quick glance and then smiles.

Bikash Roy: Capt B.D. Kapoor, why are you in such a hurry to hang Ramchandra? You will get your chance in the witness box. Your turn will come. (*He goes to the witness box*) Subedar Saahab, I have nothing more to ask you. I was needlessly arguing with you. Ramchandra has admitted that he opened fire without giving a challenge. Your eyes and ears are fine. Absolutely fine. But I have a suggestion. Do give it a thought. Why did Ramchandra open fire? Why did he kill? Sometimes the truth crouches silently in the dark, like a cat. Look carefully, and you see it.

Subedar bows his head. He walks wearily away from the witness box and sits in his place. He is lost in thought. A murmur rises in the courtroom but subsides as Surat Singh looks around sternly. The guard in the arched doorway moves, but checks his step.

Surat Singh: A break for five minutes. You may all go out. (*Looking at Capt Roy*) You stay back.

The guard comes out of the arched doorway. The people file out of the courtroom and the tread of their boots is heard. The guard returns to the arched doorway. He stamps his feet audibly. Bikash Roy is standing in front of Surat Singh.

Surat Singh: Capt Roy, what are you up to? Why did you indicate to Ramchandra that he should confess that he had fired without challenging the officers? You have tightened the noose around his neck. Why? For God's sake, why?

Bikash Roy: Sir, I do not want to save Ramchandra on technical grounds. Everyone knows that he fired the shots and committed murder. The question is: why did he open fire? Why did he kill? I am not here to save Ramchandra, no one can save him.

Surat Singh: You could try, at least.

Bikash Roy: Sir, I am trying to save something that is even more precious than Ramchandra's life.

Surat Singh: What?

Bikash Roy: Truth. Truth, which is more valuable than even human life.

Surat Singh: (*Surprised*) What are you? Are you a lawyer or...?

Bikash Roy: (*Sadly*) I am a hunter of the soul.

Surat Singh: (*Surprised*) You may go out, Captain...

Bikash Roy exits. Surat Singh takes his pipe to his lips but then puts it down. He looks at the Judge Advocate and says:

Surat Singh: He does not speak our language. Hunter of the soul, indeed! What the hell does it mean?

Judge Advocate: We should be wary of Capt Roy. He uses language like a weapon. I think the Law Department at Army Headquarters has thought deeply before sending him to this court martial. It is the first instance after Independence of a soldier killing his officer. Do you recall General Puri's case? He was sentenced to life imprisonment. Roy was the prosecutor in that case and I was the defence counsel. Roy's arguments led to the sentencing. He knows how to get to the truth. Nothing stops him. No one can emerge unscathed from his trap. Indeed, he is the hunter of the soul.

First Judge: But he is the defence counsel in this case. How will he save Ramchandra? In fact, he has made Ramchandra confess that he fired his weapon without challenging the officers.

Judge Advocate: The question is not how he will save Ramchandra, but who else he will kill.

Second Judge: One thing is sure, he is always smiling. He does not lose his cool.

Judge Advocate: Yes. A smiling tiger. A tiger in cover always smiles when he sees his prey approaching. He knows there is no way the prey can escape. No way at all. The smiling tiger!

Third Judge: (*To Surat Singh*) May we all go out for a while?

Surat Singh nods. The Judge Advocate, along with the other judges, leaves the room. Surat Singh fills his pipe, takes a long drag and exhales slowly. He walks to the arched doorway, then turns and walks around the room, talking to himself.

Surat Singh: (*Taking a deep breath*) The smell of the enemy. The smell of wartime. The smell of danger. In the last war, when I charged the enemy post with just three jawans, the aim was clear: kill or be killed. That time, I had smelt the enemy. The bandolier of grenades around my neck and the heaped corpses of the enemy. But here, in this court martial, there is no battlefield. So why do I smell danger? (*He reaches Bikash Roy's vacant chair*) Is the captain an enemy? (*Shaking his head*) No. (*Lost in deep thought, he stands in the *arched doorway where the guard was posted.*) But the enemy is lurking somewhere. If I can smell danger, the enemy can't be far away. (*Harshly*) But no enemy has escaped Surat Singh. Never! Never, ever!

Surat Singh comes out of the room. A dim light falls on the four windows. Each window frames a face—a talking face.

First Face: No one can save Ramchandra now. He will hang, for sure.

Second Face: This Bengali captain is hand-in-glove with the prosecutor and the State. Why did he get Ramchandra to confess that he had opened fire without a challenge? Officers always help officers; the rich always help the rich.

Fourth Face: But this Bengali captain is not afraid of Col Surat Singh, whose very name sets people trembling. And he did corner the Subedar!

First Face: It was all a big farce. There was only one way to save Ramchandra, and Capt Roy first showed the way and then blocked it. Why?

Second Face: We are being fooled in this stage-managed battle for justice.

Third Face: At last the truth has emerged. Capt Roy has tightened the noose around Ramchandra's neck.

Fourth Face: What is this 'hunter of the soul' business? Where does the soul figure in a legal battle? This Bengali captain is a tiger lurking in cover. A tiger has no friends. The tiger must hunt his prey. Capt Roy is the hunter and Ramchandra is his prey.

The light moves away from the windows. The guard takes his place in the arched doorway. One by one, people enter the courtroom. Col Surat Singh is last to enter. Everyone stands up. Surat Singh takes his chair and everyone sits down.

Maj Puri: My next witness is Capt B.D. Kapoor.

Capt Kapoor thrusts his chest out and enters the witness box.

Maj Puri: Capt Kapoor, have you ever taken any action against Ramchandra?

Capt Kapoor: No, sir!

Maj Puri: Did Ramchandra ever complain against you?

Capt Kapoor: No, sir.

Maj Puri: On the night of the murder, did Ramchandra challenge you?

Capt Kapoor: He opened fire without challenging us.

Maj Puri: (*To the court*) I have nothing further to ask.

Surat Singh: Your witness, Capt Roy.

Bikash Roy walks around Capt Kapoor and goes and stands in front of Surat Singh.

Bikash Roy: Sir, I do not wish to cross-examine Capt Kapoor now. But I should be granted permission to call him later.

Surat Singh: All right. Maj Puri, call your next witness.

Kapoor returns to his seat.

Maj Puri: My next witness is the regimental doctor, Capt Gupta.

Capt Gupta enters the witness box. He looks confident.

Maj Puri: Where were you on the night of the murder?

Dr Gupta: I was returning from the mess on my scooter, trailing the motorcycle of Capt Verma and Capt Kapoor. As I turned away towards my quarters, I heard the gunshots. Immediately, I rushed to the spot.

Maj Puri: What did you see there?

Dr Gupta: Capt Verma was lying on the ground. I checked his pulse and found that he was dead. The bullet had hit him in the neck. Capt Kapoor was unconscious and bleeding profusely. His pulse was weak. I took off my shirt, ripped it and tied it around his shoulder to stop the blood. Otherwise...

Maj Puri: Where was Ramchandra then?

Dr Gupta: Five jawans were holding on to Ramchandra but he was struggling to free himself, shouting, 'Leave me alone, I'm going to kill Capt Kapoor!'

Maj Puri: What happened after that?

Dr Gupta: Subedar Saahab had already called up the military hospital from the guardhouse. The ambulance arrived in five minutes. We put Capt Kapoor in the ambulance and I sat by his side. The bandage slipped from his shoulder and I tied it on again to stop the blood. We took Capt Kapoor straight to the operation theatre. Surgeon Col Joshi had already reached there. He said that if I had not bandaged the wound in time, Capt Kapoor would surely have died.

Maj Puri: Did Capt Kapoor go into surgery right away?

Dr Gupta: No. He was first given a blood transfusion. Luckily, his blood group was the same as mine (*swelling* *with pride*). I gave my blood to save the life of Capt Kapoor. Then he was operated upon. One inch lower, and the bullet would have pierced his heart. Luckily, Ramchandra's aim was not fatal. Col Joshi has recommended my name to Army Headquarters for a citation. For rising to the occasion at once and saving the life of a brother officer.

Maj Puri: Thanks, Capt Gupta.

Maj Puri goes back and sits down. The Judge Advocate looks at Bikash Roy. Bikash Roy gets up, walks slowly past Capt Kapoor's chair and up to Dr Gupta.

Bikash Roy: Capt Gupta, from where did you graduate in medicine?

Dr Gupta: From the Armed Forces Medical College, Pune. I'm a gold medallist.

Bikash Roy: Great. Congratulations! On the night of the murder, did you yourself hear Ramchandra shouting, 'Let me go! I will kill Capt Kapoor!'?

Dr Gupta: Yes, I heard it with my own ears.

Bikash Roy: But why was he shouting? Had he gone mad that night?

Dr Gupta: (*Sarcastically*) Capt Roy, that's a figure of speech. There is a difference between a madman and a man mad with anger. Ramchandra had gone mad with anger. (*In an arrogant voice*) Don't think you can trap me. I am not Subedar Balwan Singh.

Bikash Roy: (*Smiles*) Great! Congratulations! You should have been a lawyer instead of me. Anyway, why was

Ramchandra admitted to the Military Hospital five months ago?

Dr Gupta: Ramchandra had contracted typhoid. I had referred him to the Military Hospital myself.

Bikash Roy: How did you learn that he had typhoid? Did you have his medical report with you?

Dr Gupta: No. He did not report sick. That day, our regiment had a hockey game with the air force team. Ten minutes after the start of play, Ramchandra collapsed and fainted.

Bikash Roy: Was he running a temperature?

Dr Gupta: More than 104 degrees! I called up the Military Hospital and asked for an ambulance. I had diagnosed typhoid, and the medical test at the hospital confirmed it.

Bikash Roy: Great! Congratulations! How could your diagnosis ever go wrong! After all, you won a gold medal at the Pune Medical College. All right, you're a great doctor. The hockey match started at 4 pm and ten minutes later Ramchandra fell unconscious on the ground. Tell me, can a fever rise to 104 degrees in just ten minutes?

Dr Gupta: No. Typhoid fever does not rise as rapidly as malaria fever. Ramchandra must have had a temperature even before the match.

Bikash Roy: Did you not know before the match that he was running a temperature?

Dr Gupta: How would I know? I had not checked the temperature of the players before the match.

Light laughter in the court. Even Surat Singh looks at Bikash Roy and smiles.

Bikash Roy: (*In an apologetic voice*) Dr Gupta, please don't be annoyed by my questions. I know nothing about medicine. With your help, perhaps I may learn something. According to you, one cannot detect fever without a thermometer?

Dr Gupta: No, one can check the pulse of a patient for an estimate but the exact temperature can be read only with a thermometer.

Bikash Roy: Thanks, Dr Gupta. Thanks a lot for guiding me.

Bikash Roy turns to Capt Kapoor and stares at him for a moment. Capt Kapoor lowers his eyes. He walks around Capt Kapoor's chair and walks briskly towards the witness box. Dr Gupta is leaving the witness box.

Bikash Roy: Stop, Dr Gupta! I want to ask you some more questions.

Dr Gupta: Oh, I thought you had finished.

Bikash Roy: (*Speaking quickly*) On the day of the match, at what time was Ramchandra brought to you to report sick?

Dr Gupta: (*A little scared*) The time to report sick is nine o'clock.

Bikash Roy: That is not what I'm asking. A havildar and two jawans had brought Ramchandra to you. They were wearing watches too. Try and recall at what time they brought Ramchandra to you.

Dr Gupta: I don't remember the time. (*He looks at Capt Kapoor, his eyes scared.*)

Bikash Roy: If you want, I shall summon Havildar Raj Singh to depose here. He will help you recall the time. Was Ramchandra brought to you before or after the match?

Gupta bows his head. He wipes the perspiration from his forehead with his arm but does not answer.

Surat Singh: (*Angrily*) Captain, will you answer the question? Don't be dumb!

Bikash Roy: All right, let's forget about the time Ramchandra was brought in. (*Consolingly*) It is not necessary that you note the time when a person reports sick.

Bikash Roy walks to Capt Kapoor's chair and, raising his voice, asks the next question from there.

Bikash Roy: When Havildar Raj Singh and two jawans brought Ramchandra in, who was sitting with you?

Gupta looks all about him with helpless eyes and remains silent.

Surat Singh: (*Roars*) Answer the question, Captain!

Dr Gupta: Capt Kapoor was with me at that time.

Bikash Roy: Did you check Ramchandra's temperature with a thermometer?

Gupta bows his head again. He is silent.

Judge Advocate: Capt Gupta, you cannot evade questions by remaining silent. I am afraid that you may have to face proceedings under Army Act 39 for behaviour unbecoming of an officer. Is that clear to you?

Dr Gupta: Sir, Johnnies pretend to be sick all the time. That is why I did not check with the thermometer...

Bikash Roy: (*Cutting him short*) What is this word, 'Johnnies'?

Dr Gupta: Sir, jawans are often called Johnnies.

Bikash Roy: Capt Gupta, why do you 'sir' me? We are of the same rank. You must be aware that before Independence, British officers used to call the Indian jawans 'Johnnies'. It was a derogatory word. It was abusive. But never mind. If you prefer to call jawans 'Johnnies', who am I to stop you? But how did you guess, without checking his pulse or using a thermometer, that Johnny Ramchandra was lying? How did you decide that he was pretending to be sick? You are not a doctor, you are God! Truly God!

Dr Gupta: (*Screams*) I did not check the pulse, I did not use a thermometer, because Capt Kapoor told me that there was nothing wrong with Ramchandra. He was just shamming sickness.

Bikash Roy: Who is the doctor, you or Capt Kapoor? Capt Kapoor told you in English, cursing as he did so, not to use a thermometer. Havildar Raj Singh heard him. He can understand a little English. Tell me, what did Capt Kapoor say?

Dr Gupta: 'This bastard is shamming. Nothing is wrong with him.'

Bikash Roy: Great! Thanks, Dr Gupta. You received a gold medal for being the best doctor. It is not for me to tell you that you should not have agreed with Capt Kapoor. Capt Kapoor is not a doctor, but you are one. He said that Johnnies are always shamming sickness and you accepted that. (*Through clenched teeth*) Now I am done with you, Dr Gupta!

Gupta is still standing in the witness box. Bikash Roy looks at him with sad eyes and returns to his place and sits down. Nearly everyone in the court, including the judges, are looking at Dr Gupta with contempt.

Judge Advocate: Capt Gupta! Return to your place. Why are you standing here? There are no more questions for you.

Dr Gupta slowly walks towards his chair.

Surat Singh: No! The cross-examination is not over yet. Come here, Mr Gold Medallist. Listen! Start looking for a civilian job straightaway. And forget about that bloody citation!

Dr Gupta walks slowly back to his place and sits down. There is silence in the courtroom. The guard at the arched doorway steps forward. The sound of his boots is heard. He is staring at Capt Kapoor. His finger is on the trigger of his gun. Frightened, Capt Kapoor looks away from him and at the others in the court, as if seeking their help. Everyone is staring at him. He bows his head. The guard marches up to Surat Singh.

Guard: Sir, will you have tea here or in the anteroom?

Surat Singh: (*Getting up*) In the anteroom. The court will break for ten minutes.

Surat Singh walks out and other officers follow him. The guard clicks his heels as each officer exits. But when Capt Kapoor passes him, he remains still. Capt Kapoor stops.

Capt Kapoor: Aren't you supposed to salute when an officer passes?

Guard: (*Through clenched teeth*) Shall I show you how you should be saluted?

Capt Kapoor stares coldly at the guard, but then his shoulders droop. He walks out. The light falls on the faces conversing in the window. In one window, Capt Kapoor is seen lost in thought. Bikash Roy is seen in another, his face expressionless.

Capt Kapoor: Vikas! Why don't you drop in at my place this evening?

Bikash Roy: My name is not Vikas. It is Bikash. Why should I come to your place?

Capt Kapoor: We'll sit together and have a drink.

Bikash Roy: I don't drink.

Capt Kapoor: Never mind! We'll have some other fun.

Bikash Roy: What sort of 'fun' are you talking about? Are you talking about a woman? Your wife has not been living with you for several months. Is there someone else?

Capt Kapoor: What are you saying? *Yaar*, we are both officers. Talk politely...

Bikash Roy: No. Every criminal is my enemy. I neither talk to criminals, nor sit with them.

Capt Kapoor: (*Angrily*) Criminal? I was the one who was shot, and you call me a criminal! You will not be able to touch me. Forget it. Am I the murderer, or Ramchandra? You are an officer, but you don't know how to speak to another officer.

Bikash Roy: (*Stressing every word*) Capt Kapoor, forget this bloody brotherhood of officers. You know very well who the murderer is. Then why are you so scared? There are some questions one has to ask oneself, not others. And listen, don't cross my path hereafter, and don't try to talk to me again.

Capt Kapoor: Don't threaten me! I have seen so many like you.

Bikash Roy: (*Smiling*) Really? Do you know Bangla?

Capt Kapoor: (*Surprised*) No. Why do you ask?

Bikash Roy: (*In a poisonous tone*) In Bangla, there is a saying that if a tiger touches you, it leaves at least seven wounds behind.

Bikash Roy and Capt Kapoor's faces move away from the windows. Some other faces are seen.

First Face: Who is being court-martialled? Capt Roy is exposing everyone. Why?

Second Face: It is Ramchandra's court martial, of course. But only those who have black souls get exposed like this.

Third Face: How does the soul figure in the matter? It is not the soul that matters in court, but the evidence. And the evidence is clearly against Ramchandra.

Fourth Face: Is Bikash Roy really a hunter of the soul? Is he hunting sin, crouched in dark corners? Is he the tiger lurking in cover?

First Face: Why does he keep going around Capt Kapoor's chair so dramatically? Even the guard did not salute Capt Kapoor? Why?

All Four, Together: Which guard? The one who stands outside or the one inside? The guardian of truth who stands before the soul? That guard allows no lies to pass that way. Never!

The light leaves the windows. People enter the stage in semi-darkness and take their places. The stage is lit up.

Judge Advocate: Now the Commanding Officer of the regiment, Col Brajendra Rawat, will appear as witness.

Rawat walks slowly to the witness box. He looks worried.

Maj Puri: Sir, did Sawar Ramchandra ever complain against these two officers?

Rawat: No.

Maj Puri: Did these two officers ever complain against Ramchandra?

Rawat: No.

Maj Puri: What is the record of these two officers like?

Rawat: Very good. Excellent!

Maj Puri sits down. The Judge Advocate looks at Bikash Roy. Roy stands up. He comes and stands in front of Rawat.

Bikash Roy: Sir, you just said that Ramchandra had no enmity with these two officers. Then why did he fire on them? Had he gone mad that night?

Maj Puri: (*Stands up*) Capt Roy cannot ask this question. If he wants to take the insanity plea...

Bikash Roy: When did I mention temporary insanity? If anyone needs to plead insanity, it is you, not I.

Maj Puri: I need to plead insanity! Have you gone mad?

Surat Singh: Maj Puri! Mind your language. You know very well that Ramchandra was examined medically before the proceedings of this court martial started. Do not interrupt Capt Roy.

Maj Puri: But sir...

Surat Singh: Sit down. Continue, Capt Roy.

Bikash Roy: Why did Ramchandra fire at these two officers? Why did he kill?

Rawat: I don't know.

Bikash Roy: Why didn't Ramchandra shoot any other officer? Why did he not kill someone else?

Rawat: I don't know.

Bikash Roy: (*Surprised*) You know nothing. Surprising! You live in such a blissfully innocent world! Congratulations!

Rawat: (*Angrily*) What do you mean, Captain? Are you trying to blame me?

Bikash Roy: No, of course not. How can you be blamed in any way? You know nothing. (*To himself*) Something is rotten in the state of Denmark.

Judge Advocate: (*Sardonically*) Capt Roy, is that a question?

Bikash Roy: No, sir. I just recalled a line from Shakespeare's *Hamlet*. (*Turns to Rawat*) Sir, I have seen Ramchandra's confidential report. You have given him an A-Plus. Why? What special quality did you see in him?

Rawat: Ramchandra was one of the smartest soldiers of the regiment. He was diligent and honest. An ideal soldier.

Bikash Roy: Did Capt Kapoor ever lodge a complaint against him?

Rawat: No. I have never received any complaint against Ramchandra from anyone.

Bikash Roy: When you went to the parade ground on March 7, what was happening there?

Rawat: A parade, what else?

Everyone is smiling, except Surat Singh. Bikash Roy circles around Capt Kapoor's chair and then returns to stand in front of Rawat.

Bikash Roy: Sorry, sir. I did not frame the question properly. Perhaps you do not remember, but on that day Capt Kapoor had punished Ramchandra, making him salute a hundred times!

Rawat: Yes, I was going towards the golf course. I was surprised to see all the soldiers standing at attention. I went there to see why they were not marching. Ramchandra was saluting. Subedar Saahab told me that Capt Kapoor had punished him.

Bikash Roy: What did you do then? Did you inquire?

Rawat: Why? I have complete faith in my officers. If Capt Kapoor saw that Ramchandra had not saluted him properly, he must have seen right! It is an officer's right to mete out punishment.

Bikash Roy: You're right, sir! But why did you order Capt Kapoor to return every salute? He had to return the salute a hundred times!

Rawat: (*Sternly*) Captain! Don't you know the rule? If an officer is in uniform, he has to salute back.

Bikash Roy: (*Smiling*) Sorry, sir! I did not know of this rule. We in the legal department are unfamiliar with these fine traditions of the army.

The people in the court look at Rawat with pride. But Capt Kapoor does not look up.

Bikash Roy: All right, sir! Why did you order an extra daily ration of two kilograms milk and almonds for Ramchandra?

Rawat: (*Wistfully, as if recalling a scene*) It was the Raising Day of our regiment. Ramchandra came first in the 5,000 metre race. His timing surprised me. He clocked just twenty seconds more than the army record. I realized that he could break the record. That is why I sanctioned the extra rations for him.

Bikash Roy: Congratulations, sir! Not many officers have such a discerning eye! Did Ramchandra prove himself worthy of your expectations?

Rawat: Absolutely. In the Northern Command Games, he clocked just five seconds over the army record!

Bikash Roy: Did he break the army record?

Rawat: (*In a disappointed tone*) Why only the army record? Ramchandra could have broken the Asian record! But this mishap took place before the Inter-Command competition. He would have won the Asian gold medal for us. My regiment's Ramchandra would have been the fastest runner in Asia!

Bikash Roy: All right, sir. Who was the 5,000 metre champion before Ramchandra?

Rawat: (*Surprised*) Why? What does this question mean?

Judge Advocate: Col Rawat, you can't argue with the defence counsel. Just answer his question.

Bikash Roy goes to Capt Kapoor's chair. Rawat looks at them both. A knowing look appears on his face.

Rawat: Capt Kapoor was the 5,000 metre champion before Ramchandra.

Bikash Roy walks swiftly to Rawat.

Bikash Roy: Why did Capt Kapoor lose this race?

Rawat: How would I know? How the hell would I know? Sometimes you ask stupid questions, captain!

Bikash Roy: (*In a conciliatory tone*) Sir, please don't be angry. The answer to my question is quite simple. Behind every victory is a defeat with its head hanging low. Capt Kapoor lost this race because Ramchandra ran faster than him!

Maj Puri: Capt Roy should be prevented from asking such questions. Who won the race and who lost it has no bearing on this court martial.

Bikash Roy: (*In a low voice*) It does have a bearing. You know very well, and so does everyone in the court, that it does have a bearing on the court martial. But no one is willing to face it. Who are you to prevent me from asking questions? You are not the presiding officer of this court martial. Why do my questions unnerve you? Why are you afraid? Is the truth knocking at the doors of your soul?

Surat Singh: (*In a teasing tone*) Capt Roy, you talk so well of the soul and God and whatnot. Which god or goddess do you worship?

Bikash Roy: I worship Kali. Blood-sucking Kali! Kali who drinks the blood of evildoers! Thousand-armed Kali!

Stunned silence in the court. Everyone looks fearfully at Bikash Roy. The guard at the arched doorway changes his position. The sound of his boots breaks the silence. Bikash Roy moves from Kapoor's chair to stand in front of Rawat.

Bikash Roy: Sir, where is Kapoor's wife these days?

Rawat: How would I know? Ask Kapoor.

Maj Puri: Capt Roy cannot ask questions about anyone's personal life. He has no right to defame anyone.

Surat Singh: How is he defaming anyone? There are no journalists here. The whole proceedings are in camera. In the army, privacy has its limits. If a foreigner stays in an officer's house, he has to report the matter to the commanding officer. If someone has a drink too many, it has to be reported to the CO too. There is no such thing as a totally personal life in any army of the world! Continue, Capt Roy.

Bikash Roy: (*To Rawat*) Sir, why isn't Mrs Kapoor living with her husband these days?

Judge Advocate: Why are you asking him this question?

Bikash Roy: Sir, a CO is a father figure—he is like the head of the regimental family. And a happening in the family is never personal. (*Turning to Rawat*) I shall help you recall the fact that Capt Kapoor's wife had come to see you in your office a month before this crime. What was her problem?

Rawat: (*Angrily*) How do you know that she met me a month before the crime? Are you God?

Bikash Roy: One does not have to be God to know the truth. All one needs is a little transparency. Capt Kapoor's wife is in Delhi at her parents' home. I met her. She even gave me a copy of the letter she had given to you. What had she written in that application?

Maj Puri: Capt Roy has no right to defame anyone. This court martial is not being held because of Capt Kapoor's wife. It is being held because Sawar Ramchandra committed a crime, a murder.

Surat Singh looks at the Judge Advocate, whose head is bowed. He looks at Kapoor, whose head is also bowed. He looks at Bikash Roy, who is walking slowly, shoulders slouched. He is like a tiger getting ready for the kill.

Surat Singh: Capt Roy, do your questions have any bearing on the case? If they do, then continue with the questions. (*Turning to Maj Puri*) Listen, Major, do not interrupt again and again. Understood?

Bikash Roy: I shall not ask the CO Saahab any other question. I shall just narrate the complaint Capt Kapoor's wife made against her husband. When Capt Kapoor returned from the mess that night, he was drunk. Or, rather, dead drunk. When he went to his wife, she left the bed. She said to Capt Kapoor, 'Don't touch me. You're drunk. You're stinking. Don't touch me!' But Capt Kapoor was too drunk to pay any heed. He tore his wife's nightgown and said, 'I have the licence to sleep with you. Just lie down quietly. Don't you know who I am? I am Kapoor.' At which his wife said: 'Just touch me and see what happens! See if I don't complain to the CO this time!' Kapoor was out of control. He slapped his wife and screamed, 'Is the CO your father? Is he your lover? You would complain to the CO, you...' He picked up an ashtray from the table and hurled it at his wife's head. It struck her near the ear, bursting the eardrum. She fainted. The drunk Capt Kapoor did not realize that his wife had been so badly hurt.

Surat Singh: (*Stands up and roars*) You have crossed every limit, captain! Were you there in the room that night? Speak up! How in hell do you know what happened that night?

Bikash Roy: I was not there that night. But someone else was—an eyewitness to this incident.

Surat Singh: Who?

Bikash Roy: Ramchandra. He was Capt Kapoor's orderly at the time. He took Mrs Kapoor to the hospital. I may be lying, Ramchandra may be lying, but not this paper. This is a photocopy of the application Mrs Kapoor gave to the CO. She has written that her husband is a sadist. An animal. She is at her parents' home in Delhi and has filed for divorce. She has charged him with animal behaviour. Here is her divorce case file. (*Gives the papers to Surat Singh.*)

Rawat: (*Surprised*) But I was told that she got hurt because she slipped and fell down.

Bikash Roy: Yes, sir! It is always like that. Only the wife slips, never the husband. The kitchen fire, too, is wise. It catches the daughter-in-law, never the daughter. Perhaps you do not know what she told the CO of the hospital. He was all for transferring the case to the civilian police, but some officers of the regiment prevailed upon him not to do so. You can imagine the consequences had the case gone to the civilian police. The army's name would have been tarnished. The scandal was suppressed. But Capt Kapoor's wife is a brave woman. She has refused to accept further torture. She has demanded a divorce. She has told the court that her life is in danger from her husband, Capt B.D. Kapoor. If the court permits me, I can call as witness the hospital CO and other officers who intervened to cover up the incident.

Capt Kapoor: (*Rising angrily*) Bikash Roy! You are a Naxalite! Your elder brother too was a Naxalite. He was killed in a police encounter. There is sedition in your blood. You are defaming the army. You are a bloody Naxalite! You belong to a family of murderers. You...!

Surat Singh: (*Roars*) Captain, sit down!

Capt Kapoor: No, I will speak out! I will speak! (*Spittle runs freely from his lips.*)

Surat Singh: Guard! Make the captain sit down!

The guard marches up to Capt Kapoor, grabs him by the shoulders and pushes him down into his chair.

Capt Kapoor: (*Jerking the guard*'s *hands away*) Don't you dare touch me! Don't touch me.

Guard: (*Raising his rifle to his shoulder threateningly*) Sit down! Sit!

Capt Kapoor looks up at the gun. He sees the guard's inflamed face and sits down. The gun is still at the guard's shoulder.

Surat Singh: Guard! At ease!

The guard turns towards the arched doorway, but stops. He turns and looks at Capt Kapoor with burning eyes. Then he quickly returns to his post.

Surat Singh: (*Stands up*) The court will meet tomorrow morning at nine.

Darkness descends on the stage: End of Act One.

Act Two

The lights come on. Everyone is seated in his place, only Bikash Roy is standing. Everyone is looking at Bikash Roy as though they are waiting for him to answer the charges made against him by Capt Kapoor.

Bikash Roy: Capt Kapoor was right. My elder brother was a Naxalite and died in a police encounter. My brother was a dreamer and dreamt great dreams. Those who try to realize such honest dreams never die their own death. They always die at the hands of others. It is also true that I fight the same battle for justice as my brother. The only difference is that while my brother fought with a gun, I fight armed with the law. My family has been fighting this war for justice for hundreds of years. Perhaps Capt Kapoor does not know that though my brother was a Naxalite, my father is a judge at the Calcutta High Court. (*He walks slowly to Capt Kapoor*) And Capt Kapoor, you have not unravelled a great national secret! Before a person joins the army, the police verify his family background and character. Not only are the police aware of all this, so is the Indian government. (*Laughing*) Still, I was given a commission in the army. And now I have been sent to fight a case against an officer like you. Perhaps that is why you're so angry with me.

Maj Puri: I request the court not to put Capt Kapoor's outburst on record. He said some unnecessary things in anger and nervousness. He is tense. After all, he is a human being.

Bikash Roy: Really! Is he? Do you mean that in his rage Capt Kapoor does not realize what he is saying or doing? Maj Puri, even if someone loses his senses, his balance of mind, the fight for justice will carry on.

Maj Puri: It seems you are fighting on the wrong side this time. You are fighting for a murderer!

Bikash Roy: It is not for you or I to decide this issue. That is the privilege of the honourable court. It is for the court to ponder why a simple and disciplined soldier shot his own officers. Why? All human beings are alike, aren't they? But if one human being behaves like an animal, a wild animal, the other will have to take up a weapon in self-defence. This is bound to happen. Perhaps Sawar Ramchandra feared that Capt Verma and Capt Kapoor could make a fatal assault on him. When all escape routes were closed, he took up the sword. (*Bikash Roy faces Capt Kapoor*) If this man can assault his wife and injure her grievously, who knows how he must have treated Sawar Ramchandra, to the extent that he was provoked into taking up the gun. When it is cornered and in danger, even the docile cow lashes out with its horns. And Ramchandra is merely human—a simple man who was forced to take a life to save his own.

Bikash Roy sits down in his chair. He looks tired and sad.

Maj Puri: Are you trying to prove that Ramchandra was so scared by the hurling of the ashtray that he opened fire? On the night of the killing, the two officers were not armed.

Not even a fork or knife on them. This court martial is being conducted on the basis of evidence. The truth stares one in the eye. Yet you are trying to call it self-defence. This court martial is not for discussing why and when and who became an animal. Capt Roy appears to be reading a paper at a seminar on psychology, rather than acting as a defence counsel!

Bikash Roy: (*Stands up*) You are right, Maj Puri. Absolutely right. I should not be talking thus. We are all here to search for a small truth. And I got to talking about the long battle for a much larger truth. Sorry! I am really sorry. (*Looks at Surat Singh*) I pray to the court to call Subedar Saahab to the witness box again. I have some questions for him.

Surat Singh asks something of the Judge Advocate, who nods. Surat Singh looks at Subedar Balwan Singh. The Subedar gets up and comes to the witness box. He looks tense and frightened.

Bikash Roy: (*In a soothing voice*) Saahab, please don't think that I have recalled you in order to harass you in any way. You know very well that a subedar is a bridge between the soldiers and the CO, the bridge through which the complaints of the soldiers, their joys and sorrows, reach the CO. The CO too follows the same route to reach out to the soldiers. You are the source for all information on them. Why, I hope I am not saying anything wrong.

Subedar stands silent. His head is bent. He nods: yes.

Bikash Roy: Saahab, when CO Saahab ordered the extra diet of milk and almonds for Ramchandra, was he serving as an orderly in Capt Kapoor's home?

Balwan Singh: No, sir! CO Saahab ordered the extra diet for Ramchandra when he won the 5,000 metre race on the Raising Day. Ramchandra was made an orderly in Capt Saahab's home afterwards.

Bikash Roy: CO Saahab had ordered a special diet so that Ramchandra could prepare for the Northern Command games. And you put him on orderly duty. Why? Why did you do that?

Balwan Singh: Sir, it was Capt Kapoor who ordered me to put Ramchandra on this duty.

Bikash Roy: Did you not inform him that the CO wanted Ramchandra to prepare for the race?

Balwan Singh: Sir, Capt Kapoor told me that he would help Ramchandra prepare for the race. He would run with him in the mornings and evenings. He had been the 5,000 metre champion. I thought he was right. So...

Bikash Roy: Would Ramchandra come to the grounds for practice after becoming an orderly?

Balwan Singh: Yes, sir, he came.

Bikash Roy: Good! How many times did he come in a month?

Balwan Singh: (*Speaking softly*) Twice or thrice.

Surat Singh: Saahab, speak out loud. Loudly! The court must hear what you are saying.

Balwan Singh: He came two or three times a month.

Bikash Roy: Wasn't it wrong for him to come for practice just two or three times, especially when the CO had sanctioned extra rations for him?

Balwan Singh: Yes, sir!

Bikash Roy: You must have made some inquires. Did you take any action against Ramchandra?

Balwan Singh: I inquired from Ramchandra, and he told me that at the time of practice Capt Kapoor would assign him some household chore or the other.

Bikash Roy: Saahab, what are the duties that an orderly is supposed to perform?

Balwan Singh: According to the rules, he is supposed to keep the officer's uniform in order and clean his weapons. But you know...

Bikash Roy: Yes, I do know. Rules and laws are only for the unimportant and the meek. What do the big and powerful think of rules? An orderly becomes a personal servant of the officer. He has to do the shopping, take the children to school, cook and serve, iron the Memsaahab's clothes and keep Saahab happy all the time. It is not your fault! You can take action against your juniors, but you cannot complain against your seniors.

Balwan Singh: But sir, I relieved him of the orderly duty before the Northern Command competition. And Ramchandra won the race with just ten days of practice.

Bikash Roy: Good! Very good! Did you remove him from duty on your own, or did someone ask you to do so?

Subedar hangs his head and does not answer.

Surat Singh: Saahab! Answer the question. Did the CO order you to remove Ramchandra from orderly duty?

Balwan Singh: No, sir. Ramchandra complained to me.

Bikash Roy: What was his complaint?

Balwan Singh: Sir, you know Ramchandra belongs to a low caste. Capt Kapoor used to call him, '*Oye*, Harijan!' Ramchandra requested me to change his duty or else he would take his complaint to the CO Saahab's durbar.

Bikash Roy: (*Surprised*) And you accepted his unnecessary complaint? So what if Capt Kapoor called him Harijan? Harijan was a word given to the lower castes by the Father of the Nation, Mahatma Gandhi. To call Ramchandra a Harijan is not to abuse him. You should not entertain such useless complaints soldiers make against their officers.

Balwan Singh: No, sir! It isn't like that.

Bikash Roy: (*Quickly*) What was it, then? What was Ramchandra's complaint?

Balwan Singh: Sir, Ramchandra said that Capt Saahab abused him. He addressed Ramchandra as choohrha and bhangi in public. His friend Capt Verma would call him 'choohrhe da puttar'.

He hangs his head in shame.

Bikash Roy: So what did Ramchandra do?

Balwan Singh: He refused to work in the house.

Bikash Roy: What courage, that a soldier should refuse to work in an officer's house! You and the CO Saahab have already said that Ramchandra never shirked duty. Did you take any action against him for refusing to work?

Balwan Singh: No, sir!

Bikash Roy: Why not?

Balwan Singh: Sir, one day it went too far.

Bikash Roy: What went too far?

Balwan Singh: One day some guests had come to Capt Kapoor's house. A little girl did potty in the drawing room. Capt Saahab asked Ramchandra to clean it, but he refused.

Bikash Roy: What is 'potty'? Don't use slang.

Balwan Singh: Shit! Ramchandra refused to clean the little girl's shit! At this Capt Kapoor said in front of the guests, 'A choohrha by caste and too good to clean shit! Your forefathers carried our shit in baskets on their heads.' (*The Subedar's voice trembles.*)

Bikash Roy: Ramchandra could have made all this up.

Balwan Singh: No, sir. Ramchandra never lied, and I myself have heard Capt Kapoor abuse him in this manner many times.

Bikash Roy: Did you report all this to the CO?

Balwan Singh: No, sir. I thought that I would sort it all out. It is best not to let such filthy talk spread.

Bikash Roy: You thought right. Anything indicating injustice should not be spread. The powerful always oppress us. But what you do not know is that a small injustice leads to a bigger injustice. If you had brought all this to the notice of the CO, perhaps the murder could have been prevented, and this court martial too.

Balwan Singh: (*Sounding defeated*) I thought...

Bikash Roy: You thought right. The government is foolish in appointing a colonel CO. The government should make the Subedar the CO! Am I not right?

Balwan Singh: (*In a repentant tone*) Sir, I am at fault. I should have reported all this to the CO. Perhaps the murder could have been prevented.

Bikash Roy: (*Sarcastically*) No, the murder could not have been prevented. You were not at fault, Subedar Saahab. The rules of the system are such: Suppress the complaint of a small man and shut your eyes to the faults of a big man. You made no mistake. You may return to your place. I have no further questions.

Subedar walks slowly to his seat, his head bowed, and sits down.

Bikash Roy: Sir, I wish to question Capt Kapoor.

Judge Advocate: Now, the eyewitness to the crime, Capt B.D. Kapoor, will appear as witness.

As Capt Kapoor walks to the witness box, the guard at the arched doorway receives a piece of paper from a soldier. The guard reads it, marches to Surat Singh and clicks his heels.

Guard: Sir, you have been called to the telephone.

Surat Singh: Answer the telephone call and bring me the message.

The guard goes to the soldier, talks to him and returns.

Guard: Sir, it's only for you.

Surat Singh: Where is it from? Who wants to talk to me?

Guard: Sir, Delhi. Army Headquarters. General Saahab!

Surat Singh: (*Rising from his chair*) A two-minute break.

He follows the guard offstage. Some people stay seated. Seeing Bikash Roy starting to walk out, Kapoor hurries up and goes out before him. The stage is darkened and the lights fall on the windows.

Capt Kapoor: (*His face is seen from the second window*) Stop, Capt Roy. I want to talk to you.

Bikash Roy: (*From the third window*) Yes?

Capt Kapoor: You can defame me all as you want, but you can't save Ramchandra from the gallows. Never! Never!

Bikash Roy: I told you I don't talk to criminals. Get lost!

Capt Kapoor: Criminal? How can I be a criminal? (*Angrily*) You bloody...!

The light moves across to the stage. The Judge Advocate beckons the guard over.

Judge Advocate: Has Colonel Saahab answered the telephone? Any special message?

Guard: Sir, not Colonel but *Brigadier* Surat Singh! General Saahab from Delhi has himself congratulated him on his promotion.

Surat Singh enters. Everyone rises and congratulates him. Surat Singh sits down. His face is hard.

Surat Singh: This is not the place for congratulations. (*Looking at Maj Puri*) Major, start the proceedings.

Capt Kapoor: Congratulations, sir! We must celebrate your promotion.

Surat Singh: (*Smiles*) Yes, Captain! We must celebrate. We'll have a party. (*Looking at Capt Roy*) Proceed with the work of the court, Capt Roy.

Bikash Roy: (*Stands in front of Capt Kapoor and points to the medal on the latter's chest*) Why were you awarded this medal?

Capt Kapoor: I got this medal for...

Bikash Roy: Would you please speak in Hindi?

Capt Kapoor: (*Looks at Surat Singh*) Sir, I can't speak Hindi well. I may please be allowed to speak in English.

Surat Singh looks at Bikash Roy. A brief silence. Then Bikash Roy nods as though he has understood everything.

Bikash Roy: Capt Kapoor, where were you born?

Capt Kapoor: Amritsar.

Bikash Roy: And where did you study?

Capt Kapoor: Amritsar. I graduated from there.

Bikash Roy: So you are a graduate. Congratulations! I have seen your certificates. Hindi was a subject you took in your senior school and graduation examinations. But you say that you can't speak Hindi well. Strange. I was born in Calcutta and studied there, yet I know Hindi. I can speak and write in Hindi. Never mind, though. I suppose you speak to the soldiers in English. Is that so?

Capt Kapoor: I can speak some broken Hindi...

Bikash Roy: What is this 'broken Hindi'? You find it insulting to speak your own language? Is that it?

Capt Kapoor: Officers always speak in English. That's been the tradition since British times.

Surat Singh: Captain, the days of the British ended years ago, but it seems the hangover remains. (*To Bikash Roy*) We are not involved in a linguistic battle. Perhaps Capt Kapoor can express himself better in English. Let him speak in English.

Bikash Roy: Why did Ramchandra complain against you to Subedar Saahab, Capt B.D. Kapoor?

Capt Kapoor: The army no longer recruits people from a good background. When people from low castes are recruited, this is bound to happen. Complaining and shamming at every point! That is why discipline in the Indian Army is...

Bikash Roy: You need not worry about discipline in the Indian Army. But would you tell me what you mean by 'people from a good background'?

Capt Kapoor: People who come from well-off families. When the scum of the earth are recruited into the army and they get a bellyful to eat, won't their heads turn?

Bikash Roy: Their heads will certainly turn. Capt Kapoor, you are from a good background and belong to an affluent family.

Bikash Roy: Yes. For the past four generations my family have been rulers. They are officers of the civil service, the foreign service, the army, navy and air force. We belong to the ruling class.

Bikash Roy: You have a big and weighty family tree.

Capt Kapoor: (*Puffing out his chest*) Yes, I'm proud of it.

Bikash Roy: You should be. You should be proud of it. What did your father do?

Capt Kapoor: He retired as a deputy inspector-general of police.

Bikash Roy: But he could not become an inspector-general.

Capt Kapoor: (*Angrily*) DIG isn't a low rank either.

Bikash Roy: No. Not at all. But he was suspended twice in five years.

Capt Kapoor: So what? Nothing could be proved against him. He emerged with flying colours.

Maj Puri: (*Stands up*) Sir, Capt Roy has no right to defame anyone's parentage. Who exactly is being court-martialled? Capt Kapoor, or his father, or Jawan Ramchandra?

Bikash Roy: I shall not ask such questions. I shall not ask them again. I was just trying to understand what a 'good background' is. (*To Capt Kapoor*) For some time now, your family has been living in Delhi, not with you. You must be dining at the mess.

Capt Kapoor: No, I eat at home. A maid cooks for me.

Bikash Roy: Perhaps your memory is failing you. For several days you have not been dining at home or in the officers' mess, Capt B.D. Kapoor.

Capt Kapoor: (*In a sharp tone*) Yes, I have not been eating there. I have been eating at my friend Capt Verma's home. Is it a crime to eat at a friend's home?

Bikash Roy: No, of course not. When did I say it was? All right, Capt Kapoor, nowadays officers get free rations, don't they?

Capt Kapoor: Yes, they do. So what?

Bikash Roy: If you dine at a friend's house, what do you do with your free rations?

Capt Kapoor: I give the free rations to my servants.

Bikash Roy: No, not to the servants. For several months you have been sending your orderly to sell the rations at the shop of Banwari Lal and Sons in Sadar Bazaar. Should I present Lala Banwari Lal or your servant as witness? Should I present witnesses to prove that you sell the government rations, Capt Kapoor?

Capt Kapoor: Other officers too...

Surat Singh: (*Roars*) Don't talk of other officers. Does your orderly sell the rations or not?

Kapoor bows his head.

Surat Singh: I get the feeling that I could be court-martialling you next.

Bikash Roy: (*Looks at Surat Singh*) Sir, there may be no need to wait for the next court martial. (*Turns to Kapoor*) Why did you lose to Sawar Ramchandra in the 5,000 metre race, Capt B.D. Kapoor?

Capt Kapoor: Before he joined the army, Ramchandra was a goatherd. He chased animals all day.

Bikash Roy: No, that's not it at all! You are the superman. You know why you lost the race. (*Spitting out each word*) You were defeated because you had been drinking day and night. Seeing your mess bill, the CO had warned you twice. When you lost to Ramchandra, your pride in your 'good background' and your ego were deeply bruised. You became his foe and started insulting him.

Capt Kapoor: Me? And Ramchandra's enemy? Enmity

is possible only with equals, not with small people. You're talking a lot of bullshit.

Bikash Roy: Who are these 'small people'?

Capt Kapoor: Small people are small people. That's all.

Bikash Roy: Ramchandra belongs to the category of small people. Isn't that so? Did you call Ramchandra a choohrha and bhangi, Capt B.D. Kapoor?

Capt Kapoor: No. He has been lying. And anyway, if you call a bhangi a bhangi, is it a crime?

Bikash Roy: (*Stressing each word*) It is no crime, Capt Bhikhari Das Kapoor?

Capt Kapoor: (*Screams*) Call me B.D. Kapoor!

Bikash Roy: But your full name in your school-leaving certificate is Bhikhari Das Kapoor. You know why your mother gave you this name? You were born late in her marriage. Your family believed that if one had to wait long for the birth of a son, he must be given a humble and small name. Bhikhari Das Kapoor!

Capt Kapoor: (*Screams*) I am B.D. Kapoor. Don't call me by any other name.

Bikash Roy: If you can call a bhangi a bhangi and a choohrha a choohrha, why can't I call you by your real name, Bhikhari Das Kapoor?

Capt Kapoor: Stop it, or...

Bikash Roy: Or what? Will you slap me like you slapped Ramchandra when he objected to being called a choohrha? Will you hit me like you hit your wife when she called you a jerk? Impotent, cruel animal!

Capt Kapoor: (*Screaming in rage*) You bastard! You son of a bitch! I'll kill you!

Capt Kapoor snatches the gun from the guard. Everyone stands up, horrified.

Capt Kapoor: Seed of a dog! I won't let you live.

Surat Singh: (*Stands up and roars*) Captain! Put the gun down!

Everyone is stunned. Kapoor looks at Surat Singh.

Surat Singh: Didn't you hear me? Put down the gun this moment!

Kapoor puts down the gun and sits down right there on the floor.

Surat Singh: Come on, get up and go to your place.

Capt Kapoor walks listlessly to the witness box. The Colonel looks at the people, who are still on their feet.

Surat Singh: Take your seats. (*Turns to Bikash Roy*) Capt Roy! You may put a question to him if you so wish.

Bikash Roy: (*In a sad voice*) No, sir. I don't want to ask him anything more.

Judge Advocate: (*Looks at Capt Kapoor*) Capt Kapoor, take your place.

Capt Kapoor leaves the witness box and walks, completely defeated, to his chair. His head is bent low. The guard picks up the gun from the floor and stands alert, pointing it at Capt Kapoor.

Surat Singh: Guard, at ease!

The guard points the gun away from Kapoor and returns to his post. The Judge Advocate looks at Maj Puri.

Judge Advocate: Do you want to present any other witnesses?

Maj Puri: No, sir.

Judge Advocate: If the defence counsel wants, he can call a witness. Yes, Capt Roy, do you wish to produce any witnesses?

Bikash Roy gets up and stops for a moment near Kapoor, and then goes to Ramchandra. Ramchandra looks at him and lowers his head. Bikash Roy continues to look at him. Ramchandra raises his head and looks up at him. Bikash Roy points to the witness box. Ramchandra goes and stands in the witness box. Bikash Roy looks at Surat Singh and the latter nods in approval. Bikash Roy goes to the witness box. Before he can ask a question, Ramchandra starts speaking.

Ramchandra: (*Looks at Surat Singh*) Sir, I won't answer any questions. I have killed and I should be punished.

Surat Singh: You will be punished.

Bikash Roy: What is your name?

Ramchandra: Sir, I won't answer any questions.

Bikash Roy: (*Surprised*) I have not asked any questions. I have just asked you your name. Your name is Ramchandra. You were named after the deity who fought for justice. That is why your parents must have given you this name.

Ramchandra: Sir, I do not know why my parents gave me this name. But Capt Kapoor used to say that every other choohrha-chamar is named Ramchandra these days. However, I shall not answer your questions. I have already confessed that I killed Capt Verma.

Bikash Roy: (*Angrily*) So do you want a Paramvir Chakra for committing murder? Do you want me to garland you? Do you want me to worship you? You will be hanged. That is what is done to a murderer. Why are you so proud of being a killer? You think you are a great hero? You were not afraid when you murdered a man, but you are afraid of answering questions. Even if low-caste people like you are given equal rights by law or the Constitution, it makes no difference. You will remain fearful, timid and cowardly. After swearing to speak the truth, you are too shy to speak at all! I think Capt Verma and Capt Kapoor were right when they called you choohrha-chamar, Ramchandra.

Ramchandra: (*Stands erect*) Sir, don't abuse me. I won't answer any question.

Surat Singh: Ramchandra! You are an important member of our regiment. The regiment is proud of you.

Ramchandra: Thank you, sir!

Surat Singh: We are not your enemies. Tell us precisely what happened. You have lived bravely, now you must learn to die bravely too. Tell us truthfully: what did these two do to you?

Ramchandra: They would hurl filthy abuse at me.

Bikash Roy: What did they say?

Ramchandra: They would call me choohrha-chamar

and bhangi. They would mock my light skin by calling me chitta-choohrha!*

Bikash Roy: You had not challenged them that night. So why did they stop the motorcycle near the sentry post?

Ramchandra: Sir, whenever I was on guard duty, they would stop and curse me. They were angry because I had asked the Subedar Saahab to relieve me from orderly duty.

Bikash Roy: What sort of abuse did they hurl at you that night?

Ramchandra: It was very foul.

Bikash Roy: (*Screams*) What was it? You have sworn to speak the truth. Speak out!

Ramchandra: (*Screams*) Chitte-choohrhe! A bitch-born bastard! Your mother must have slept with a Kapoor or a Verma!

His scream turns into the cry of a wounded animal. He bends slowly and sits down, his head almost touching the floor. He is weeping loudly. Silence all around.

Surat Singh: Guard, get some water.

The guard brings a glass of water. CO Brajendra Rawat takes the glass and puts it to Ramchandra's lips. The water spills. The CO puts one hand under Ramchandra's arm and raises him. Ramchandra gradually gets to his feet. He takes the glass of water and drinks it. His body is still racked by sobs. Some water spills. The CO takes the empty glass from Ramchandra, who is now standing stiffly at attention.

---

* Chitta: fair-skinned.

Rawat: Ramchandra! Men do not weep, ever.

Ramchandra: (*In a choked voice*) Sorry, sir!

Bikash Roy: (*Stands in front of Surat Singh*) I have nothing more to ask.

Surat Singh: (*To Maj Puri*) Maj Puri! Do you have any questions?

Maj Puri: (*Stands up*) No, sir!

Surat Singh: Ramchandra, return to your place.

Surat Singh confers with the Judge Advocate, who nods in affirmation.

Judge Advocate: Maj Puri! Closing statement.

Maj Puri: When Ramchandra himself has confessed to the crime, there is nothing left for me to prove. Capt Bikash Roy tried his best to prove that Ramchandra had been tortured and abused. Even if he had been tormented, our society, which is based on rules and laws, provides for other means of protest. But no, Ramchandra could not see any other way. He could see only one way: to kill. There is no place in society for personal anger and revenge. Absolutely no place. Ramchandra could have complained to his Commanding Officer. He could have complained to the Army Chief. He could even have complained to the supreme commander of the defence forces, the President. But he did not. Even if we are to accept that these two officers abused him, harassed him, it is only a moral offence. Ramchandra, on the other hand, resorted to the worst crime: killing another human being! Abuse does not merit a bullet. Ramchandra has killed. He is a murderer. Thus, under Army Act 69 and Section 302 of the Indian Penal Code, he should be hanged by the neck until dead. Nothing short of the death sentence would be adequate penalty for this crime.

Maj Puri sits down. After a brief pause, Bikash Roy gets up.

Bikash Roy: (*Speaking softly*) The prosecutor has rightly stated that our society is based on law and systems. And society has no place for protest by a single individual. No room at all. Yes, society has devised ways for voicing protest but these paths are long. One can walk them, but the question is: do they lead anywhere? Absolutely not. They go nowhere. Protest is not a play where one must wait till the last act. Protest by the powerful is known as political protest and it takes them, in one leap, very close to the seat of power. But protest by the weak takes them, again in one leap, to the gallows. When small protests are ignored and swept under the carpet, a terrible reaction is inevitable—a violent outburst.

The law and the Constitution have given equal status and rights to all citizens. But the upper class has not given these right to the lower class, the rich man has not given these rights to the poor. A society which follows the system of caste, of the high and the low, is fragile.

Why talk of equality, when we do not allow those smaller than us the right to think, to look us in the eye? The reason for all this is our way of thinking and living, the feudal tendencies that we are still not rid of.

He stops and sighs. Then he speaks loudly.

Bikash Roy: The prosecutor is right. Sawar Ramchandra should be hanged until dead. The soldier who had pledged to guard his country refused to clean the shit of a little girl! The soldier who had pledged to guard his country refused to be called a bastard! The soldier who had pledged his life to his country refused to shut his eyes! He must be punished. The death sentence! Yes, he must be sentenced to death under the Army Act and Section 302 of the Indian Penal Code. He must be sentenced to death again and yet again!

Bikash Roy sits down, short of breath. There is complete silence. Surat Singh looks round the room. The Judge Advocate leans towards him and says something.

Surat Singh: All of you, please clear the room.

One by one, all exit. Now, only the judges remain. The guard is standing by the arched doorway. Surat Singh looks at the judges.

First Judge: Life imprisonment!

Second Judge: Life imprisonment!

Third Judge: Death sentence!

Fourth Judge: Death sentence!

Surat Singh looks at the Judge Advocate.

Judge Advocate: Sir, I can't advise you.

Surat Singh: So the deciding vote will be mine. My vote will decide between life and death. Good! (*Orders the guard*) Guard! Call in Ramchandra, his CO and the two lawyers.

Guard: Yes, sir. (*Goes out.*)

Ramchandra, Rawat, and the two lawyers come in. Bikash Roy draws Maj Puri to a corner and discusses something with him. Maj Puri nods.

Surat Singh: I shall announce the court's decision at nine tomorrow morning.

Surat Singh rises and descends from the platform. Maj Puri clicks his heels.

Maj Puri: Sir, I have a request. Please transfer Capt Kapoor out of this regiment. His life is in danger. He may also be issued a revolver until his transfer orders come through. Capt Kapoor should be ordered to keep the revolver with him at all times.

Surat Singh stops in front of Bikash Roy, then he moves on to Col Rawat.

Surat Singh: Col Rawat, issue a revolver to Capt Kapoor right away.

Rawat: Yes, sir! I hope you remember that it is the day of the burra khana. Two celebrations today—the Raising Day of our regiment and your promotion to the rank of brigadier.

Surat Singh: Yes, I remember, Rawat. I shall certainly come. Listen, allow Ramchandra to come to the burra khana. Any problem?

Rawat: No problem, sir! By all means, sir.

Surat Singh: Ramchandra, tonight you shall be my guest. You *will* come to the party, won't you?

Ramchandra: (*In an emotional voice*) Yes, sir! I'll certainly come!

Everyone leaves the room. The guard comes to centre stage, not marching any longer but walking at ease. Ramchandra goes up to him. The guard puts his hand on his shoulder and the two walk out in a friendly manner.

Darkness.

People enter the dimly-lit stage. A long table is covered with white linen. A flower vase adorns the centre of the table. A tray with rows of glasses is on the table; they are filled with rum. People are standing in a corner, chatting. Capt Kapoor enters and the guard tells him:

Guard: Sir, please park your car in the parking lot. No car should be outside the door. Those are the CO's orders.

Capt Kapoor: (*Handing him the car keys*) You park the car. I'm late.

Guard: Park it yourself. I'm not anyone's servant. I serve the Government of India.

Capt Kapoor: Talk properly. You know the punishment for disobeying an officer's orders? I shall report you.

Guard: (*Derisively*) Don't mistake me for Ramchandra! I never miss my aim. I serve the Government of India!

Capt Kapoor's shoulders droop. He walks away unhappily. Sound of laughter from a group. Surat Singh goes to the table to put down his empty glass. Capt Kapoor walks in smartly and goes to the Colonel. He offers his hand.

Capt Kapoor: Congratulations on your promotion to brigadier!

Surat Singh: (*Staring at him, and his hand*) How dare you try and shake hands with me! Get lost! Don't let me see your face as long as you live.

Capt Kapoor lets his hand fall. He walks out like a dead man. Surat Singh picks up two glasses from the table and walks up to Ramchandra. A gunshot is heard outside. People run out after the guard to see what has happened.

Ramchandra: Sir, something has happened outside. Should I go and see?

Surat Singh: I know what has happened.

Ramchandra: I don't understand, sir.

Surat Singh: When the courts of the world fail to deliver justice, the Old Man up there intervenes. (*Offering him a glass*) Come, have a drink.

Ramchandra: Sir, I don't drink.

The guard enters and goes to Surat Singh.

Guard: Sir! Capt Kapoor has shot himself! He has committed suicide.

Surat Singh: Ramchandra, are you afraid of death?

Ramchandra: No, sir. Ramchandra fears no one.

Surat Singh: Tomorrow I am going to sentence you to death. I have nothing but a death sentence to give you.

Ramchandra: (*Thrusting out his chest*) I happily accept whatever you give me.

Surat Singh: Will you not drink even now? The last drink with me?

Ramchandra: (*Gratefully*) I will drink. I certainly will. Thank you, sir!

Surat Singh and Ramchandra clink glasses. Ramchandra downs his drink in one shot.

Surat Singh: Thank you, Ramchandra!

Curtain.

ALSO FROM SPEAKING TIGER

A Bouquet of Dead Flowers

Stories

Swadesh Deepak

Translations by Jerry Pinto, Pratik Kanjilal, Nirupama Dutt and Sukant Deepak

Among the most uncompromising of modern Hindi prose writers, Swadesh Deepak's unsettling stories have a profound ability to offer a searing critique of society, of bureaucracy, but also to upend the usual masculine stereotypes found in much literature of our time.

The little boy in 'Hunger' who scrounges for leftovers by the station is pleasantly confused by the godown guards' generosity one day when his sister tags along. The Prime Minister's imminent visit to their small town, in 'No News of Untoward Events', is too disruptive for the residents to cause much excitement. In 'Name a Tree, Any Tree', the headstrong Maya Bakhshi can't make sense of her family's kindness towards Major Ajay Singh, until she does, and the ground slips beneath her feet. Sunila, in 'Horsemen', falls in love with the unnervingly quiet Sukant, who runs mad whenever it snows. There's an unspoken tension between Naveen and Nimmi in 'Dead End', but the generous hosts at the hotel they've come to during this unusual time of the year could never guess why. And in 'The Child God', the Pandit and his family find out just how depraved they can be.

'Hindi literature, Swadesh Deepak maintained, had to be forced out of its comfort zone,' writes Jerry Pinto in his Introduction. 'The reader here is treated no less savagely.' The stories in this volume will challenge and shake readers and hold them in their grip for a very long time.

ALSO FROM SPEAKING TIGER

I Have Not Seen Mandu

A Fractured Soul-Memoir

Swadesh Deepak

Translated by Jerry Pinto

> '[Deepak's] searing account of his seven-year battle with mental illness...[is] a one-of-its-kind book in the annals of Hindi literature.' —Poonam Saxena, *Hindustan Times*

When Swadesh Deepak—celebrated Hindi playwright and short-story writer—arrives at PGI, Chandigarh, after having tried to set himself on fire, the doctors don't know if he belongs in the burns unit or in the psychiatric ward. He's living a 'curse'. A dangerous seductress—his Mayavini—is taking revenge for his insulting rebuff at her wish to visit with him the famous lovers' palace in Mandu. She comes to him at night, sometimes with three white leopards, and she leaves the smell of her body in his nostrils. When he tries to kill himself, she tells him he will not die. He is firmly in her clutches, but he will tolerate anything for her, from humiliation at the hands of acquaintances to carnivorous worms under his skin.

This fractured, shattering narrative—among the most unusual books ever published in India—records Deepak's descent into madness and his brief, uncertain recovery. Shortly after it was published, he left home for a walk one morning and never returned. As the translator, acclaimed author of the path-breaking *Em and the Big Hoom*, writes in his introduction: '[Deepak's] words carry all the scars of who he was and what his illness had made of him... His voice echoes from the bottom of a well.'